LET IT RIDE

Jay Cronley

ECHO POINT BOOKS & MEDIA, LLC

Published by Echo Point Books & Media
Brattleboro, Vermont
www.EchoPointBooks.com

Let It Ride
ISBN: 978-1-63561-826-6 (paperback)

Cover design by Kaitlyn Whitaker

Cover image: *"Thoroughbreds Racing for the Finish"* by Sara Julin Ingelmark,
courtesy of Shutterstock

"My name is Greenberg," a man in the box said, extending his hand to Trotter, "and I got more goddamn money than I know what to do with. My philosophy is, nobody knows you got money, what the hell is the use of having it?"

"Bernie is so silly," a blonde said.

Bernie Greenberg said to Trotter, "This is Miss Backstretch," of the blonde. Trotter waited for the punch line and when none came, he took the blonde's fingers.

"I'm pleased," she said.

Trotter said nothing.

The blonde's breasts said it all. They were about to explode through a flimsy white blouse. The force of this eruption would send buttons flying to the far corners of the Jockey Club.

Trotter cleared his throat eventually and said he didn't know they had a beauty contest at the track here, but he assumed it must be quite an honor to have won.

"He thinks you won a beauty contest," Bernie said.

"I could of, I think," the blonde said.

"And if you didn't, I would have bought it," Bernie said.

Funding for most of the research involved here was provided by a modest Daily Double grant one fine spring afternoon in 1978 at Oaklawn Park in Hot Springs, Arkansas. A horse named Rambunctious Road made this novel possible by winning the first race.

TROTTER AND LOONEY GOT OUT OF THE CAR and turned the keys over to a guy who wore an Indy 500 ball cap and a black-and-white checkered shirt.

"It's hell out there," the guy said, nodding at the parking lot where other guys wearing ball caps were spinning tires and broadsliding Cadillacs and Lincolns into nooks and crannies almost invisible to the naked eye.

Most eyes were covered.

Several people who had handed their keys and cars over to these daredevils were sobbing. Others had their fingers over their eyes and were peeping through the cracks and listening for glass.

It cost seven dollars to park in this lot directly across the street from the track where horses race. For that sum, you were given a claim check with the terms of the parking agreement on the flip side. Management was not responsible for windshields that burst due to the heat. Management was not responsible for theft of anything from a hubcap up

1

to and including the theft of the actual car.

Trotter carefully studied this one-sided contract. The guy under the Indy 500 ball cap said, "You're probably wondering what management *IS* responsible for."

Trotter jumped. It was mildly depressing to have your mind read by a man with six teeth.

"Yeah, I was," Trotter admitted. "Wondering."

"Management is sorely responsible for making good change," the guy in the ball cap said, taking Trotter's ten. "Seven take away ten is three." Trotter was given three ones and a smile. The guy looked like a Halloween pumpkin, with those teeth.

"Management is also responsible for upkeep of the facility."

The lot appeared to have once been gravel, but most of it had been flung into the street by spinning tires. A sign said that according to an ordinance, no more than three hundred cars could be parked on the lot. Yellow lines had been painted so that when the parking lot inspector made his rounds, he would find three hundred neatly squared-off spaces. The only trouble was, you could step across the yellow lines.

Seven dollars times three hundred cars is $2,100 a day; times six racing days a week is $12,600; times twelve racing weeks is $151,200.

That's a lot of money, Trotter thought. That's an enormous, fantastic lot of money. It's a dream.

"So is seven dollars," Looney said.

Trotter jumped again, and frowned.

"I read your lips," Looney said. "You went, that's a lot of money, with your lips."

Trotter handed the claim check back to the attendant. "I won't need this."

"Why?"

"Because I'm giving you the car."

2

The guy in the ball cap began blinking quickly. He paused to direct a fellow daredevil toward the back of the lot. The kid skidded an Olds into a space about the size of the box it came in, and then crawled out of the driver's window.

"You're giving me the car to PARK, right?" the guy in the ball cap asked Trotter. "Jake" was over his pocket.

"No. I'm *giving* you the car. It's yours. I'm sick of it. It's got a rattle in the right side and the glove box won't shut. I just decided. Give me the seven bucks parking fee back. Take the car."

The guy in the ball cap looked from Trotter to Looney to Trotter to Looney, who shrugged and said, "He's been known."

"Now just wait a minute," Jake said, adjusting the bill of his cap. "You're GIVING me this car."

"He's a millionaire," Looney said. "If you don't want the car, give it to your girl friend."

Looney asked if Jake had ever heard of Colonel Sanders.

"Well, Jesus Christ, yes. Everybody has."

"That's his nephew, Lieutenant Sanders."

"Well, Jesus Christ."

Looney said, "Gives a car a week away. Sometimes two."

"Christ."

"Just remember this," Trotter said. "Be generous. It's the secret of life."

Jake looked across the street. For a second he thought he was on "Candid Camera." There had to be a catch. Nobody gave anything away around here except bad advice. But then he had read where Elvis used to give away Cadillacs to people like old ladies, so maybe there was a God. Maybe this *WAS* his lucky day. One thing, he was due.

3

"Well, hell, thanks," he said, looking at the keys. "I mean, this is real nice."

"Just remember," Trotter said, "this is America. Anything can happen to those who go to Sunday school."

"I ain't been to church in twenty years. But I'll start. I swear to God, I'll start. I promise."

Trotter told Jake how to get the glove box shut and he quickly showed him the lever that washed the windows. "Generosity is good for the soul."

"Oh yeah," Jake said.

Some tourists got out of a new Chevy and one of Jake's chums got behind the wheel and stomped the gas pedal. Wisps of smoke rose from the pavement. The Chevy made a right turn at the end of a row and was backed into a stall designed for little red wagons.

The cars were parked so close together, the parker couldn't get out of the window. The owner of the Chevy watched what happened next with his hands on his head.

"Watch this," Jake told Trotter and Looney. "Gilbert invented this next move. He's the best I ever saw at it."

Gilbert moved the Chevy forward out of the alleged space. He got out of the car and walked around the front and squinted one eye, sighting the fender of the Chevy back into the parking space.

"He's lining her up," Jake said. "There's no margin for error in this one."

When all appeared well, Gilbert twice got on his hands and knees to take measurements, the kid shoved the Chevy backward with his foot. The car was in neutral, and it went into the parking space like a quarter going into a slot machine. The Chevy gently bumped a car parked behind it. Gilbert crawled up on the roof of a station wagon and reached his skinny

4

arm through a space in the Chevy's window, and put her in Park. He swaggered to the front of the lot and gave a claim check to the owner of the Chevy, who was mopping his brow with the collar of his shirt.

"Gilbert is the greatest there is at that maneuver," Jake said. "That's why we pay him $1.80 an hour. He used to work across in the bus lot. Once, he foot-rolled a Greyhound into a spot the size of a Buick. They let the kid go, though, over there, when he backed a bus over one of them portable johns with an old man in it. We snapped Gilbert right up. A lot of guys, they peel off a little paint, they get cautious and play it safe. Gilbert, that one is fearless. Has the guts of a burglar."

"Also the morals of one," Looney said.

Gilbert was over on the back row, trying a few trunks.

"Speaking of Buicks," Jake said, "I can't thank you enough for giving me this one."

Jake went into his front right pocket and came up with a twenty, which he gave Trotter, who took it. Trotter said Jake didn't have to do that.

"You know what they say about being generous," Jake winked.

"That's the spirit," Trotter said.

Trotter pocketed the twenty and told Jake to take care.

"Come back," Jake said. "Any time. I mean it. I'll be here."

Trotter and Looney crossed the street in front of the track.

"Happy motoring," Trotter shouted to Jake, who took his Indy 500 ball cap off and waved it. The lot was full, but cars were being parked in the aisle. Trotter had once parked in a similar lot down the street. His Buick was placed snugly on the back row, and after the races, he was one hour climbing in the window and two hours getting to the street. He was able to get out so quickly because he and the man in the Corvette to the left removed a fence and backed through somebody's garden.

Jake got in Trotter's, Trotter's hell, *HIS* Buick and waited patiently while Gilbert removed a car from the front row. The front row is where your people who tip approximately twenty dollars get their cars parked. Your car is on the front row, all you have to do is drive over a curb and you're free. All the cars on the front row were expensive. Jake waited while Gilbert removed a Jaguar and backed it in figure eights to row four where it was casually parked in the middle of some lousy Toyotas. Gilbert checked the trunk on the Jag, shrugged, and peered around for somewhere to put a motorcycle a guy just brought in.

Jake meticulously inched Trotter's, rather *HIS,* Buick into a spot on the front row. It went in smooth as you please.

Jake tenderly opened the driver's door so it wouldn't lose a paint chip. He cracked the window an inch, so it wouldn't blow up because of the heat. He squinted at the hood and wiped off a bug spot from the windshield with his elbow. He stood back by the curb and admired the black Buick. He nodded his head. It was a keeper, all right. He pitched the keys in the air, caught them, and put them in his right front pocket. He saw Trotter and Looney observing the proceedings from across the street. He waved again.

Those guys waved back.

They were smiling.

Damn, Jake thought. You pay your dues long enough, God smiles on you. DAMN, this day has got a good ring to it. He decided to take the seventy-five dollars he had rat-holed to get a new fuel pump for his 1969 Ford and bet it on the blackest horse in the first race. By dusk, the way things were going, somebody would be parking *HIS* car. DAMN!

"Appreciate it," he shouted at the two guys.

"It's low on gas," Trotter shouted back.

"Appreciate it."

Trotter and Looney watched as Jake stopped a rumpled old man on the sidewalk. Jake took some keys and gave them to the old man. After some discussion, the old boy drove an old Ford off the lot. They waved at each other.

"I think he just gave away his car," Looney said to Trotter.

"Looks as if," Trotter agreed.

They walked to the main gate. Trotter had the other key to the Buick in his left shoe so nobody would steal it.

Twice, some track rat snatched a brown paper sack from Trotter's hand.

The first time, there had been a ham and cheese in the sack.

The second time, a couple of months ago, there had been nothing but a note in the sack.

CONGRATULATIONS YOU DUMB GODDAMN SNEAK THIEF, Trotter had written on a card; YOU JUST STOLE A SACK WITH NOTHING IN IT.

A person drops his guard five minutes at the track, somebody will swipe the pennies out of his loafers.

Trotter looked once more at his Buick resting comfortably on the front row, and then he and Looney discussed what they would do with the twenty-dollar windfall from Jake. Trotter decided to buy a beer, and maybe give the rest to Charity.

Shiela was working the crock game and was blessing everybody. She used to strip almost naked at

7

the Horsefeathers Friday and Saturday nights and slap bald guys on the head with her breasts, for which she sometimes received as much as a two-dollar-bill tip if the bald guy had hit a couple of winners.

The Horsefeathers is a bar across the street from the track where guys go to get hot tips before the races from Marty, who has not picked a winner since 1948, when he liked Citation to win the Derby. The thing that took the edge off Marty's 1948 selection of Citation was that some one to four million other people had similar vibes.

Trotter is one of the few citizens who frequent the track on a regular basis who would not like to see Marty hanging by the feet from the starting gate.

"Look at it this way," Trotter told Looney, who had made a less than Christian comment about the Horsefeathers and its proprietor. "Marty picks one of his winners every race."

"He picks a *HORSE* every race," Looney said, curling his lip in the direction of the Horsefeathers. "He hasn't picked a winner since 1945."

"Forty-eight. Citation. Anyway, he also picks a Daily Double and favorite and long shot of the day, right? Now, Looney, that's about fourteen horses that have the kiss of death, that you don't have to worry about."

It was true, Looney nodded. Marty gave a horse the magic touch, it could just up and die from that moment on. Trotter said it was invaluable to have the names of approximately fourteen horses that could not win a race if they went around in the back of a pickup.

"That leaves only approximately eighty-six horses to worry about," Trotter said, "in a day of racing."

"As good as that is, it's still depressing," Looney groaned. "God almighty, that's a lot of horses. It's a little scary to think of them all lumped together like that. Throw out six favorites that win that won't pay peanuts. So you have to find four ten-to-one shots out of eighty horses to win any money. That's the most depressing thing I ever heard."

Looney has a way with words. He can make "Merry Christmas" sound like it's going to be your last.

Every once in a while Looney comes up with a way to make money with little or no effort, so Trotter tunes it out when Looney lapses into his frequent periods of morbid depression that sometimes last years.

"If you can eliminate a horse a race the way Marty does, that's a big help," Trotter promised Looney.

"I guess," Looney said.

If Looney saw a twenty in the gutter, he would say, "Probably counterfeit," or "I'd get it, except my back would go out." Looney would look a gift horse in the mouth and worry about catching a cold.

THERE IS ONE OF EVERY KIND AT THE TRACK, SOMEtimes two.

You didn't see too many Salvation Army workers with blouses unbuttoned halfway down to their knees, like Shiela.

Mickey Jax was on down the road, past Shiela, playing like he knew which horse was going to win the first race. Then, he would play like he knew which horse was going to win the second race. He played smart guy ten times a day. He hit mostly the women tourists. You can tell when a person isn't too familiar with the horse racing process, and what Mickey does is spot some woman who wouldn't know the *Racing Form* from the want ads, and he gives her a horse. He gives twelve women horses, or seven women horses, or however many horses are in a race. Sometimes he tips men, but they're greedier. Mickey gives them a winner, sometimes they won't show up at the right post for the pay-off. Women, they're fair.

Say you get off some tour bus and buy a program and *Form* and sit down with a beer to figure things out. If you haven't read a *Racing Form*, it looks a lot like Chinese stock quotations with all the dates, past performances, workouts, and speed ratings. But you have heard there are guys at tracks who sleep with horses, guys who *KNOW* things like what horse has what limp where. If you stopped to think about it, you might wonder if this guy knows so much, why the hell isn't he betting the family jewels? Well, here's why. Nobody thinks much at the track. You get two beers down and it's like a dream with all the noise and people. Maybe that little guy has a crush on you or something. Mickey Jax dresses poor. His family jewels are a rubber band around his wrist and a pencil behind his ear. So there you are, having a cool one, watching the people, wondering what a speed rating is, and here comes this little guy looking like a puppy. He looks at your program and says the three horse. For sure. A mortal lock. It's just his luck, the day he gets a cinch, he's a little shy in the financial department. Now the next best thing to having money and betting it on a mortal lock is having somebody else win it, because you're all in this together. The track is the enemy and if anybody can get in its drawers, swell. So there, lady, bet the three horse. It's all yours, Mickey Jax says with a smile. Heard it from the trainer himself. The three horse, they've been holding him back in the glue races, waiting for the odds to get jacked up, so today they're turning him loose. The trainer, now this is confidential, he has got something like two grand to win on the three horse. What would be nice, Mickey Jax says, is if after the three horse wins, you might stop back here by this post and bench and slide something crisp like a ten to your old pal. That would be very white. So you wad the damn paper with the confusing numbers in it into a ball and stuff it in the trash box and bet the three horse. Your friends will be spellbound when they hear of the encounter with the character.

Sometimes the horse wins.

Sometimes he doesn't.

Some people care, but not Mickey Jax.

After he gives every horse in the race away, like he was giving away a daughter to be married, he has a beer and watches the action on an indoor TV screen.

Say three wins.

He goes back to the third post and waits for his reward.

Fortunately, there are a lot of posts under the grandstand so it won't fall, and a lot of people milling around, so the person he gave the four horse to won't spot Mickey and give him a different kind of reward, heaven. That's another thing with women. You give a man a loser, he is often prone to take Mickey's head into his own hands. With women, they're calmer.

A week back, Mickey Jax gave a fat woman from Toledo the winner in the first. She was overjoyed and hit him with a nice, crisp ten. He gave her number five in the second. *THAT* damn thing won. For his wisdom, he got twenty dollars. The woman from Toledo got four winners from Mickey, which is just short of qualifying for the Guinness records. After the last race, where Mickey gave her the nine horse, which won by nineteen lengths, skipping, the fat woman from Toledo picked Mickey Jax off the ground, swirled him around her head, and then kissed him on the mouth. What made this tolerable was she palmed him a lovely, crisp fifty in the process.

Mickey Jax likes thin ladies.

When you give somebody a winner, as opposed to a shower or placer, chances are he will hit you pretty firm with anything from a ten spot on up. Ten per cent is a good average. Say one of the dogs comes in and pays 50−1, the tourist will heap maybe fifty dollars on you. But if the favorites come in a lot, you're lucky to get the ten.

What Mickey Jax does on the busy days like today is he gives the tourists "in the money" mortal locks, like saying the three horse is a cinch to be in the top three.

What happens there is Mickey Jax gets hit three times, not as much as with a winner, sometimes, but on the average, giving "in the money" mortal locks as opposed to winning mortal locks earns Mickey about 6.5 per cent more a day.

It's a little hectic making stops by three posts, but it's the price you pay for being a race track pimp.

Say Mickey gets the minimum he asks for, for a winner—ten dollars. That's a crisp hundred and twenty dollars a day, tax-free, unless you count the way pushing through crowds taxes your patience. He works six days a week and earns about fifty grand a year being a track tout, which is not bad for an ex-jockey. It is also not bad for something like an ex-dentist. Actually, it's good.

They let Mickey Jax quit being a jockey because they caught him holding back a horse. Holding back is another phrase for fixing. Some creep of an owner paid Mickey Jax five hundred bucks to keep a horse from winning. The horse was really feeling its oats that day and tried to run away from the other ponies. At the top of the stretch, Mickey had to lean up and put his hands over his horse's eyes to slow the damn thing down, which didn't sit kindly with the stewards, so they gave Mickey Jax his walking papers.

Mickey Jax was outside the main gate having a smoke, checking out the tour buses full of widows. He looked like he just fell off a tomato truck.

"Who do you look like?" Looney asked him.

"Everybody," he answered with utmost honesty.

Trotter and Looney continued past Mickey Jax toward the general admission booths.

Mickey Jax wondered what made guys like that tick. How could *anybody* in his right mind try and make honest money off horses?

Oh well, he thought, watching an elderly woman hobble off a bus, that's what makes a horse race:

Losers.

He walked in with the old woman and gave her the one horse in the first race. Trainer. Been holding him back. Ready to run. Mortal lock.

"Tell you what," the old woman said. "I've got a bad leg. Why don't you take this twenty dollars and bet him for me and then bring the ticket back."

"Okay," Mickey said. "Sure."

It's a living.

IT WAS STILL EARLY, AN HOUR BEFORE POST TIME, SO Trotter said why didn't they go back across the street for a cool one at Marty's.

"Cool what?" Looney asked.

"Grilled cheese," Trotter answered.

A dirty old guy was standing outside the door, leaning up against the building. His eyes were closed. He heard Trotter and Looney open the screen door and said quickly, "Here, buddy, got a winner for you in the first. The eleven horse. Is a flier. Somebitch will win by sixty-eight feet. Swear it on my mother's grave."

"His mother was cremated," Trotter said.

"When?" the old drunk asked.

"Scattered her ashes over the bar. Used to date all the jockeys. Sometimes five at a time."

"You goddamn somebitch," the old drunk said. His name was Johnson.

"I never did no jockeys," a woman who appeared a hundred and thirty-five years old said. She was next to Johnson, playing the guitar, pretending to be blind.

"Johnson, you drunk," Trotter said. "There's only ten horses in the first race."

"What's that got to do with anything, you somebitch?"

"Not many people going to bet on the eleven horse in a ten-horse race."

"Oh," Johnson said. "Appreciate it. You want the ten horse?"

"Thanks anyway," Trotter said. "But I'm not drunk yet. Here, old lady. Here's a nice crisp ten for a cornea operation."

"Sit on it," the old lady said of the one-dollar bill Trotter crinkled through his fingers.

"You take requests?" Trotter asked Johnson's mother.

"Yeah." She placed her hands on the guitar.

"Cheeseburger and fries," Trotter said.

"Creep."

"The two horse in the second," Johnson said. "I swear it. The two horse. A prize."

Trotter told Johnson there was only one horse running in the second. Johnson thought a minute and said, "Well fuck, that ought to make picking the Daily Double easier."

Trotter and Looney went inside and were met by Marty coming out. He told Johnson and his mother they were bad for business and asked them to move on.

"I'm blind as a bat and can't see," the old woman said.

Marty gave her five dollars.

"But I can smell," she said.

It was a public sidewalk, so technically the Johnsons could have stayed there. For five dollars, however, the old woman would have done a handstand. She sniffed the five and wandered to another spot to earn five dollars more from some shop owner who discriminated against the fairly blind.

Marty's was full and various bums were going through the motions, like Henry Brock, who was at the bar, claiming there was chipped glass in the beer he just drank. Marty's bartender said Henry had just swallowed a few of his teeth and not chipped glass, and that it was *IMPOSSIBLE* to swallow chipped glass in Marty's.

"Why?" Henry Brock asked.

"The glasses are plastic," the bartender said.

"I'll be damned," Henry said. "Still, chipped plastic can turn a person's guts into Swiss cheese."

Henry asked was there a lawyer in the house?

Hell no.

Marty and Henry Brock settled out of court. Marty bought Henry a beer.

Some drunk rose and bet he could sing a famous score perfectly for ten dollars. Somebody called him.

"Three to two," he sang loudly.

He collected. Everybody laughed.

There was no empty table, so Trotter and Looney

15

elbowed their way to the back of the Horsefeathers, through the smoke, which hung over the tables like infectious fog, and they sat with Vibes Eberhart, there next to the jukebox.

Dolly Parton was singing hell out of things but nobody seemed to notice, except those who found significance in the fact that there was a horse named Dolly running in the fourth race. It was the first time Dolly had RUN in five weeks. She had been entered to run in races each week since then, but in each outing, she only jogged. Looney checked Dolly out in the *Racing Form* on the way to the track and concluded, "She could win, but then she might not," to which Trotter answered, "You know Jeane Dixon?"

"Who is that?" Looney had answered.

"A woman jockey," Trotter had answered.

There are many people who think that because a Dolly Parton record is playing within six hours of a race where a horse named Dolly is running, rather racing, rather *ENTERED*, well, a lot of guys think this is a sign from God, as do parents who have kids named Dolly, dogs named Dolly, or have ever seen *Hello, Dolly.* This, the affinity to bet horses with names with which you are familiar, like you had a hamster named Dilly, is why a considerable amount of win, place, and show money is bet on goats like this Dolly in the fourth race.

The serious players, however, do not rely on such fluff, such witchcraft, such tomfoolery.

Vibes Eberhart, for example, could have cared less about what was playing on the jukebox.

Vibes Eberhart drives a cab. Trotter drives a cab. Looney drives a cab. That's the way it goes. You can make as much as twenty grand driving a cab. You can spend as much as twenty-*five* grand driving a cab and supporting a wife or more. That's why you see a lot of cab drivers at the track.

Vibes Eberhart was staring toward the front door at Marty's, oblivious to the activity around him. Not fifteen yards away, two guys were playing a spirited game of five ball, which is a pool game that is a lot of fun when all you have is five balls because numbers six through fifteen have been stolen.

The pool players were calling each other profane names and threatening each other with assorted acts of violence. One guy said he would throw a glass of scalding beer in the other guy's face if he didn't quit moving the cue ball, and the other guy said, Oh yeah, you try that and I'll bash you over the head with a grilled cheese.

"Listen, I'm sorry," the first guy said.

"Hello, Vibes," Trotter said, scooting a chair back from the table. The chair leg had been chained to the table by Marty.

People walked off with everything but the sandwiches.

"I think he's dead," Looney said of Vibes Eberhart, who had his eyes closed.

Guys were holding *Racing Forms* one inch from their eyes, the smoke was *THAT* bad. A goldfish in a bowl behind the bar was floating bloated on the top of the water. A bit of ivy had crawled out of its pot and had leaped over the side, and was dead of suicide.

A few guys who had passed out were coughing in their sleep.

"Hey, Vibes," Trotter said, knocking on the table. "You got company."

A pro football game was preparing to kick off on the television, suspended high above the bar. Neither Trotter nor Looney had bets on the game. The television set had a wire screen around the tube so some

17

sore loser wouldn't heave a glass at an interception.

The reason Trotter and Looney didn't have bets down was because Trotter owed Lufkin $220 and Looney owed Lufkin $330, and what made that appalling was the fact that all they had in the world was $120.

You don't usually pour good money after bad, or bad money after good, however the saying goes.

The thing about gambling that is so appealing, in addition to control—after all, YOU get to pick—and in addition to the possibility of a nice score, is that with gambling you can make a bet even though you don't have a boot to piss in. Gambling functions on the honor system whereby a person gives his word to pay if he loses, then if for some reason he doesn't, somebody comes by and kidnaps his kid or beats up his wife or pulls his ears off, depending on what he owes.

It's a lot like Vegas and playing with chips. A chip with five dollars or twenty-five dollars stamped on it is a lot easier to bet than a five-dollar bill. It's the same with betting a C-note when you're a couple of hundred down. "Hundred" is only a word. If you had to accompany each bet with a hundred-dollar bill, a lot fewer people would gamble, and that's precisely why bookies don't demand a deposit, from trustworthy customers, that is; guys who, like cats, have nine asses to lose.

Another thing you have to remember, and sometimes it's hard, is that when you bet something like fifty dollars, what you're really betting is double that. Say you win, you win fifty dollars. Say you lose, you lose the fifty, plus the bookie's juice, ten per cent. The difference in being plus fifty and minus fifty-five is a hundred and five dollars, which is a subtle little kick in the chops, isn't it? You bet a C-note, you're looking at a two-hundred-and-ten-dollar swing.

"I like the Giants," Looney said, watching the pre-game festivities as the camera cut to the cheerleaders, one of whom was jumping an inch off the ground. The Giants were playing the Packers. Neither team had won a game since birth.

The game was pick 'em, or even with the bookies.

Trotter said it took a man with a lot of spunk to bet on the Giants, the only team in professional football with a former soccer player running first team center. Usually, the little rascals kick.

Looney said he thought he might bet a half (fifty dollars) on the Giants, just for the hell of it. Lufkin's office accepts tiny bets like fifty dollars from regulars like Looney. Looney is so regular his weekly checks are used by Lufkin to pay a maid and a half.

"I like to bet the home team in even games," Looney said.

Trotter sighed. "What home team? The Giants are orphans."

Looney swore never to bet football again after losing three hundred dollars on the Redskins when a field goal attempt with thirty-four seconds left hit the right goal post and the crossbar and then dropped short, ONE TENTH OF AN INCH SHORT!

It was amazing.

The football hung on the crossbar a full second. That wasn't as amazing as what had happened a minute before. As the Redskins lined up for the kick that could have made Looney a new man, he had said, "The damn thing will probably hit the goal post and the crossbar and be an inch short."

When it happened about exactly that way, Trotter fell over backward in his chair.

"I knew it," Looney had said.

Getting depressed *before* the bad news seemed to be Looney's way of preserving his sanity under the constant threat of financial holocaust.

"Who knows?" Looney said, getting up from the table at Marty's. "I may not lose too bad."

"You get discounts on coming close?" Trotter asked.

"He's hooked, is a junkie," Vibes Eberhart said, blinking out of his trance. "Has all the symptoms. Where am I?"

"Twenty-one," Trotter said.

"Fuck, I'll stay. Nobody beats twenty-one," Vibes Eberhart said.

"The club, Twenty-one."

"Oh," Vibes said. "In that case, gimme a fish sandwich."

Vibes looked around, took a deep breath, and recognized the atmosphere and a familiar face, the only one he could see clearly, the clock glowing in red numbers. "I am in Marty's or have died and gone to hell, one of the two."

Marty brought a round of wet ones, you can't have everything, and Trotter asked him who he liked in the first.

Marty removed a program that had been marked with lines, arrows, dots, phone numbers, recipes, circles, squares, dashes, stick figures, exclamation points, triangles, female breasts, figure eights, and catsup stains. He held it out for Trotter to see for himself.

"What's that, blood?"

"Catsup."

Trotter said he couldn't make a thing out of the mess so Marty tapped a finger at Blurred Image. "You've heard of my thirty-two stars."

"Who hasn't," Trotter said.

"Is how many you see after you bet one of Marty's horses and pass out on the concrete," Vibes said. "Thirty-two stars."

"Listen to Lionel Hampton over there. That's the last good vibe he got. A record. Well, this is a forty star. I haven't put out a forty star in many years. Blurred Image is it."

Vibes Eberhart asked what number Blurred Image was.

Trotter said number five.

"No way," Vibes said, "on earth."

Trotter got his program out and made a check by Blurred Image, but did not tell Marty what the check meant. The last time Trotter put a check by a horse, except when it was one of Marty's stars, was when Trotter was at the paddock and noticed a gelding named Foxworth spitting blood.

"Good American jockey," Marty continued. He showed Trotter selected excerpts from the *Racing Form* that could have meant anything from the horse was stepping down in class and was ready to run to the horse was *FALLING* down in class but would have to continue on to the bargain basement to find a race it could win.

Looking at the *Racing Form* was like looking at a painting of lines and drips; whereas it could represent Man's Inner Struggles to one person, it might look like a dog's breakfast to another.

Looney returned from placing his football bet on the old, familiar Giants, and he and Trotter and Marty and Vibes Eberhart watched as the Packers kicked off to the Giants and they also watched as the football hit a Giant returner on the head and floundered on the fake turf like a fish out of water. They watched as a Packer recovered on the Giant three.

Looney said nothing.

"They ought to put that soccer player in for the kickoffs," Marty said. "At least he could kick the bastard back at 'em."

The Packers scored on the first play, made the kick.

"It could be worse," Looney said.

Everybody looked at him.

"How?" Marty asked.

"They can't go for two on the conversion in the pros."

STILL, IT HAD BEEN LOONEY WHO HAD DEVISED THE plan to make a quick hundred dollars, which would finance this raid on the track whereby the C-note would be wheeled into five times that, with a little luck. You remember luck. It's good. Last night they had played cards at Lufkin's house, which is what they do most Fridays. Lufkin is a bookie, and a very good one, and that's why he lives in a house where there are five guys out front, making sure. One guy gets the car door and another guy gets the car and yet another guy is poised to get the elbow of your lady, if there is one. A fourth guy gets the door of Lufkin's townhouse. The fifth guy stands around looking brutal with his hand over his heart. Sometimes people give the guy with his hand over his heart little packages of money and he transports them safely to the gaming area, which is all of Lufkin's townhouse except the crappers. The five guys out front make sure nothing goes wrong at Lufkin's little Friday night parties. There are also butlers, maids, and women whose hips move like they were on ball bearings. Must be whores, Looney decided. There are five blackjack tables and five poker tables and guys with thin faces do the dealing. Former Vegas killers,

Looney concluded. Only Lufkin's "regulars" may attend these sessions, only guys who have been on the books a couple of years or more, only the guys who settle up on time. Trotter and Looney are welcome guests. Looney figures he has lost enough to Lufkin over the years to have financed the hot water faucet in the master bedroom's john. That's a lot of money. There is a note card behind the hot water faucet in the master bedroom's john that says:

THIS THING ONCE WAS IN BUCKINGHAM PALACE.

Lufkin's place is like a museum.

Guys who lose a little money betting football, basketball, baseball, hockey, golf, horses, dogs, tennis, politics, or religion—Lufkin once put out a line on the Second Coming of Christ—and don't settle up are not permitted to attend the Friday night card parties. No, cheapskates are not welcome. Two years ago a guy named Blush Benson came down with a bad case of the shorts and took a little vacation for his health. Blush Benson was the only person who didn't know his own nickname. When Benson was at the card table, and had jacks or better, he broke out in a big blush. The reason gamblers have nicknames is because if you called in a bet with your own name and the police had the line tapped, well, that could be a little hairy.

Benson was down approximately four hundred and fifty dollars to Lufkin and he thought some mountain air would help. One of Lufkin's associates captured Benson as he was opening the door to leave his apartment. Benson was tied to a chair and displayed in the center of the Friday night card party as an example of what happened to a guy who was not serious about settling up.

The way it usually worked was Trotter and

23

Looney would take about a hundred bucks each to the card game. They would start slow, pacing themselves, carefully monitoring their losses. Then they would panic and lose their asses. Last Friday, Looney lost thirteen consecutive hands of blackjack, betting two dollars. He computed the odds of losing fourteen consecutive hands at 475–1, and bet seventy-four dollars on the next hand.

His first card was a two. His second card was a two.

"I'm beat," Looney said.

Trotter was standing behind Looney. "Think positive," he whispered.

"MAYBE I'm beat," Looney said.

Trotter said, "Attaboy."

The dealer was expressionless. His face was thin and mean. You could have cut a cake with it. The dealer's up card was a lousy four.

"Gimme a card," Looney said.

He got a two.

"Card."

Jack of clubs.

Looney's hand added up to sixteen. He turned to Trotter, who shrugged.

"I'm good," Looney said to the dealer, who was not.

The dealer turned his hole card over, revealing a three; three-four, total of seven. The dealer began hitting himself according to the rules.

Three, total of ten.

"I'm beat."

Four of clubs, total of fourteen.

"Goddamn, where's the big cards?"

Ace of hearts, total of fifteen.

"Please, God, big card."

Ace of diamonds, total of sixteen.

"What is this, an animal rummy deck?"

Ace of clubs, total of seventeen.

Dealer stays.

"That's three aces in a row," Looney said. "I never saw that before."

The dealer blinked slowly at Looney, who said, "Well, maybe once I did."

The dealer removed Looney's seventy-four dollars like it was lint on the table.

Trotter and Looney had discussed several times, in privacy, how difficult it was to make any money playing blackjack at Lufkin's. Looney tried a variety of maneuvers before coming up with his plan for a quick, sure-fire hundred-dollar victory. Two weeks ago, the dealer had a five up, which is poor, as a rule. Looney had a face card and an eight.

"Hit," he said.

Something almost moved on the dealer's face, which would have been a little unusual because the dealer is not supposed to know what the player holds, since the cards are dealt face down. Trotter was again standing behind Looney, and thought the dealer's bottom lip jumped. Whatever happened, the dealer recovered quickly to deal Looney the queen of hearts, and bust him.

A guy named Mel playing at the same table found it unique for a player to hit eighteen with the dealer showing a five. Mel kicked Looney for taking the face card that would have given him a hand of twenty-one. Mel was tossed out on his ear.

As the guy on the door said, "We don't like violets."

What they like is lettuce.

So after about seven years of losing Friday nights, Looney came up with a vision with which to get back approximately one third of 1 per cent of the money Trotter and Looney had lost at Lufkin's.

It worked like a new car.

That means it worked once.

At Lufkin's, it's house rules. This doesn't mean there are sets of rules in operation that you won't find somewhere else. It just means that the house rules. Supreme. Both Trotter and Looney wouldn't have been surprised if the dealers had a little something up their sleeves in addition to ice water. Face it, they were a bunch of cheats. Nobody ever won at Lufkin's. What you did was win awhile, *THEN* lose it. There are very few gamblers who are able to quit a winner, unless you blackjack and die after the first hand.

It was a variation of this theme that earned Trotter and Looney the crisp C-note.

Trotter and Looney were in very poor financial shape last night. They each had fifty dollars to work with, which was nothing to sneeze at, but on the other hand it was not the kind of stake that gave a player the confidence necessary to order a drink from one of the sirens who circulated through the tables wearing bikinis. A rule is, if you get tapped out before your drink arrives, you pay; otherwise the drinks are free.

The girls occasionally pause to watch the action and whisper things like, "Win a lot of cash and take me out later tonight, you handsome bastard."

Because of that, Trotter carried the "roll," which was two fifties resting comfortably on a bevy of ones.

When one of the girls cuddled up next to Looney and stuck a breast in his ear, he was incapable of making mature decisions like whether or not to open with three queens in five-card draw.

Trotter walked briskly to a blackjack table and exposed his low-calorie roll which *COULD* have been something like eleven fifties, but wasn't.

It was two fifties and some ones.

"Now remember the system," Looney said to Trotter loud, so the dealer could hear. "Every time you win, double the bet. You have eleven fifties. You lose a hand, start betting five bucks."

"You sure?" Trotter asked.

"I'm sure," Looney said.

A redhead saw the roll and said to Trotter, "I just got out of women's prison this afternoon and am ready for a good time."

Looney got the hiccups.

Trotter said, "How neat."

Trotter casually flipped out a fifty and won with a blackjack hand of twenty.

"Do I bet a hundred dollars now?" he asked Looney, loud, so the dealer could hear.

Looney consulted a card and said, "No, you go with fifty dollars again. If you win, you bet four hundred next time."

"You sure?"

Looney explained the Flex System, which stipulated that if the first hand in a deck gave the player twenty and a winner, he made the same bet again, and if he won that, he shot four hundred dollars.

"I've been up nine days and nights working on this," Looney said. "Trust me."

The dealer was staring a hole in Trotter's head. Dealers *LOVE* system players.

Trotter bet fifty dollars more and won with a hand of fourteen when the dealer busted on twelve.

Trotter took THAT fifty.

"Now bet four hundred," Looney said.

The dealer's ears moved. Looney SAW them.

"But I haven't got four hundred dollars," Trotter said.

"You have a handful of fifties," Looney said, mock-startled.

"Those are ones, on the bottom."

"Oh," Looney said. "I'll be darned."

"So what do I do now, with the Flex System?"

Looney studied the paper where hundreds of numbers were written and said, "Thank your lucky stars."

The dealer's right eyelid started twitching. He was probably on commission and was paid according to the gross profits from his table.

Trotter asked Lufkin for the guy with his hand over his heart. Trotter gave the guy the two fifties.

"Is this a tip or what?" the guy asked.

Trotter explained that he wanted the money transported safely to the curb.

The guy who parked cars had no trouble locating the proper vehicle. It was the only cab in the lot.

Many people left in cabs. Few drove them.

"That was the quickest hundred bucks we ever made from Lufkin," Trotter said.

Looney thought a moment and said it was the ONLY hundred dollars they ever made.

Looney sank into deep, unblinking depression.

So did Trotter.

They went home. The nights they lost, they *always* stopped off for a beer. Winning was hell, it was so unusual.

ANYWAY, THE HUNDRED FROM LUFKIN'S WAS THE most they brought to the races since Looney's aunt died two years ago and left him two hundred and twenty-five dollars. Looney had taken the *Racing Form* and thrown a dart at it in the men's room, and in the first race, the dart landed on a horse named

Irish Coffee, which broke smartly from the gate and then dropped dead of a heart attack. It was the damnedest sight anybody had ever seen and there were guys in attendance, Al Birnbaum, for one, who had seen it all. After Looney's horse succumbed, Al Birnbaum remembered certain other oddities, like the time two jockeys got in a fist fight on the backstretch while riding their horses in a *RACE*, for God's sake. But whereas Al Birnbaum was ninety-three years old, and whereas he had seen some fourteen thousand horse races in his day, he had never seen anything like Irish Coffee.

"Usually, horses die in the stretch," Al Birnbaum told Looney, who wondered what to do with his two hundred and twenty-five dollars' worth of win tickets on Irish Coffee. "You don't see many croak coming out of the gate."

Looney took his tickets to the track manager's office and was informed by a gum-chewing secretary that if he didn't remove himself from the area, guards would be called. The instant replay proved conclusively that Irish Coffee hadn't perished *IN* the starting gate. Had that happened, Looney's money would have been refunded, as would the money of other supporters of Irish Coffee, approximately all nine of them. Irish Coffee went off at 80–1. Once a race has started, it is every horse for itself. Irish Coffee had taken four brisk strides.

"Bad luck," the secretary told Looney. She told him of something that would make him feel better. She read in a racing magazine that in England once, the horse leading a race by twenty lengths was sniped by a guy who had bet hundreds of pounds on the horse running second. Those who had bet on the leader were simply out of luck. Dead is dead.

"I know," Looney said. "I mailed a cousin of mine

29

twenty dollars to bet on the horse that got shot."

The day Looney's horse died, the race was all the way around the track, so they couldn't very well leave Irish Coffee there on the ground. Eleven guys dashed out and dragged the horse to the infield.

Trotter did not say it could have been worse.

"This is an easy race to watch at least," Looney had said as they put a tarp over Irish Coffee in the infield.

Marty from across the street had listed Irish Coffee as his thirty-four star of the day.

When Looney confronted him with the bar napkin with *IRISH COFFEE*, thirty-four star, circled in red ink, Marty shrugged and said Looney should have gone with his thirty-five star that race, which lived, came in second, and paid ten dollars place money.

"I thought the thirty-four star was your top pick," Looney said meekly.

"On THAT race, my best was thirty-five stars. You guys left early. The thirty-four star is for the tourists."

Marty was making a fortune with his dollar beers, the idiots parking cars were making a fortune, Shiela was making a fortune, Solly Friedman was making a fortune selling his tip sheet, Mickey Jax was making a fortune suckering tourists; everybody seemed to be doing just great except Trotter and Looney, who were the only ones they knew trying to make a buck the way God intended, the honest way, picking winners.

Shiela was making more money than anybody in town, with the possible exception of the *REAL* Salvation Army woman down at the other gate.

Shiela wore a sunbonnet and a long, ugly skirt, slit open, though, and she stood next to a pot. She was shaking a bell. People were stuffing dollars and pitching change into the pot marked *SALVATION* in large letters, and armie in very small letters. Of course, there is no such thing as the Salvation armie, but people hurrying into the track hardly ever noticed. It's amazing how many people think it's good luck giving money to poor people, Shiela told Trotter and Looney one day after the races.

"Who do you like?" Trotter asked her.

"God," she said.

TROTTER LOOKED AT THE LISTING OF THE HORSES ELIgible for the first race and it kind of reminded him of the way they named housing additions like Whispering Pines even though there wasn't a tree in sight, and the way they did that was obviously over drinks. Blurred Image, indeed! That thing ran so slow you could shoot it with a Brownie and the picture would be in focus. The only horse that made *ANY* sense was Trotter's pick, Charity. At least the names of the horses in the first race fit the occasion. The first race was for cheap claimers. A claimer is a horse you may purchase for, in this case, $4,500. Hell, Trotter thought, some Volkswagens cost more than that. The horses were:

> MYRTLE'S DELITE.
> CHARITY.
> SHY RULER.
> KLASS.
> BLURRED IMAGE.
> CHIQUITA'S BANANA.
> DREAM ROADBLOCK.
> FANCY SPARROW.
> NEUTRON NELLY.
> COUNTERFEIT.
> LO FAT.
> GUYS N DOLLS.

Charity was listed at twenty to one in the Morning Line, which is a line that comes out in the morning. Counterfeit was four to one, and as Marty pointed out, Blurred Image was, "F-f-five to o-o-one, absolutely p-p-p-perfect."

Trotter guessed Marty was blurring his speech as a little joke.

Dream Roadblock, now there's a beautiful name for you, one that rolls right off your tongue. "Where the hell's your Native Dancer?" Trotter asked.

"Dead," Marty said. He went off to service others and hand out more stars to the loyal customers.

"It's all bullshit," Vibes Eberhart said. "Every bit of it. Eleven is the winner. I'd bet my life on it."

"They have a two-dollar minimum bet," Looney said. It was the first funny thing Looney had said in years. Perhaps his fifty-dollar bet on the Giants was the cause of his frivolity. The Giants by God made a first down! It was by penalty, but ten years from now, who's to know?

Trotter ran his finger down the program to the eleven horse, the one Vibes Eberhart favored.

Lo Fat.

"What the hell is it, milk?"

"It's the winner, Trotter," Vibes said positively.

Trotter consulted the proper date in the *Racing Form*. Lo Fat was a horse, all right. A girl horse named LO N BEHOLD had given birth to Vibes Eberhart's vision after a date with FAT GEORGE. It could have been worse, Trotter thought. Lo Fat could have been named George Behold.

Trotter had a half a plastic glass of beer, spit out the chipped plastic, and studied Lo Fat's recent performance. After several minutes, Trotter said to Vibes Eberhart, "According to this, your eleven horse has a fatal disease and is losing control of its legs. If it finishes, it will be rolling."

There was a time out on the TV game—the Giants were down 10–zip—so Looney asked Vibes Eberhart how come he liked Lo Fat.

"I don't particularly like him."

"Oh," Looney said.

"But I'm betting one-fifty on his nose."

"Oh," Looney said, pretending to understand; or worse, *understanding.*

"One-fifty what?" Trotter asked.

"What I *LIKE*," Vibes continued, "is the number."

"The odds?" Looney asked. Lo Fat was a grim 5–1.

"The NUMBER," Vibes said.

"Oh," Looney said. "The number. What number?"

"Eleven. The eleven horse."

"Oh."

"It just came to me, right before you got here."

"Looney thought you were dead," Trotter said. "Or worse, like drunk."

"I was getting the number."

"Oh," Looney said.

"The number is eleven."

Trotter's headache was getting a stomach-ache, so he ordered another beer and two aspirin and two Maalox tablets, which Marty brought in about five minutes.

"That's one more beer on your tab," Marty said. "Mind your P's and Q's. You know where that came from?"

Even though nobody asked, Marty explained.

"Back in Ireland, they used to serve beer in pints and quarts, therefore the P and Q. The barkeep let the regulars keep track of their own tabs, which was done on a blackboard. A guy would write his name

33

and beside it the number of P's and Q's. The bartender was all the time saying 'Mind your P's and Q's' whenever he delivered a round."

Looney found that bit of information amazing. After watching a quarter of the Giants, that was understandable. Anything, the flies, would be interesting.

Trotter thought in here P should stand for Pockets and Q should stand for Quartz Watches, since the pickpockets damn near outnumbered pockets, but he didn't say anything because Marty was a nice guy, even if his stars were a little dull. With what he had to work with in this dump, the clientele, Marty actually did a hell of a job.

The Giants ran a trick play. The center hiked the ball to the quarterback, who handed it back to the center. The center fell forward for a gain of one yard.

Looney was listening to Vibes Eberhart explain where he got the eleven horse as the winner of the first race.

"You almost scored, Looney," Trotter said. "And would have except the Packers hadn't left the field."

The next best thing to winning was watching somebody else lose.

"I clear my mind, first of all," Vibes Eberhart said, "of everything."

Looney listened, enraptured.

Trotter started to say that shouldn't have taken long, but didn't, because you never knew when a guy might buy you a beer out of the blue.

"I get my mind like a blackboard, blank, nothing but black. Now the only way this can be done, Looney, is you can't think about a single thing. You think about the least little thing, and you see that in your mind. You understand?"

"Okay," Looney said.

"You breathe real deep. You can't think about women, nothing. Two jugs pop up, it takes about fifteen minutes to get rid of them. Now pretty soon, usually anywhere from two to five minutes, there's going to be some numbers that pop up on that blackboard, or one number, when I'm vibing horses when only a few run."

"Vibing?" Trotter said. "Vibing?"

"Getting vibes. The numbers, they just appear. Now with football and basketball and baseball where you need teams, once I get my mind blank, the names of teams appear left to right, in script letters. It's very exciting. You never know what the vibe is going to be. Like in pro football, when the D starts, you never know if it's going to come out Denver or Detroit."

"Or Dallas," Looney said, caught up in the excitement of it all.

"Exactly."

"Or Da Giants," Trotter said.

"He's being sarcastic," Looney said of Trotter's behavior.

"Now what can be a little trouble," Vibes Eberhart said, "is when you get a Reverse Vibe."

The discovery of such an event was so stunning, nobody could think of anything to say worthy of the occasion, except Trotter. "It's hot in here."

"Now a Reverse Vibe is where the numbers or letters on the blackboard change from white to red."

"Jesus," Looney said. "How creepy."

"There I was awhile, betting whatever flashed first on the blackboard," Vibes said. "And losing some. See, you can't shut it off when you get the white vibe. Sometimes it's too early. You got to wait and see if you get a Reverse Vibe. A Reverse Vibe is where like a name comes on, then like five minutes later, it turns red."

Trotter said he had heard of that, only back then they were calling it a nervous breakdown, not Reverse Vibes.

"What if it comes in red?" Looney wondered.

"Then you forget that team, that's what. You come back about five minutes later with another vibe. But see, Looney, with a Reverse Vibe on like football, there's only two teams playing, right? Well, when you get the Reverse Vibe, you go with the *other* team. A Reverse Vibe is the same as a vibe for the other team."

Looney said it sounded great.

"Been winning?" Trotter asked.

"Basically," Vibes Eberhart said. "Last week, though, there's been a green vibe creeping in sometimes between the original and Reverse Vibe."

Trotter said the time to start *REALLY* worrying was when polka-dotted elephants in cheerleaders' gear started carrying the vibes. Trotter thought Vibes's system was clearly a bunch of crap, which reminded him, "Got to go to the bathroom."

There was a guy in there, flipping coins in relative privacy, probably narrowing the field in the first race. When the guy saw Trotter open the door to the john, he jumped in surprise and the quarter he had been flipping went right into the john.

You talk about a way to start a day. There's one vibe to send a person packing, Trotter thought.

The guy couldn't decide whether to pretend Trotter wasn't there and reach for the quarter, or pretend like a quarter was chicken feed.

"Go for it," Trotter said, "I won't tell a soul."

The guy looked at the toilet, shrugged, and said forget it.

NOBODY was that hard up.

When the guy had left, Trotter flushed the toilet and when the water receded, the quarter was stuck to the bottom of the stool. Trotter reached down for the coin.

At that moment, Vibes Eberhart opened the door.

Trotter looked up, his arm still reaching for the quarter in the toilet.

"What are you doing?" Vibes asked.

"Fishing for money," Trotter said. "I was born with a quarter in my mouth. It just came out."

THERE IS NOT MUCH THAT SEPARATES A WINNER FROM a loser. It can get pretty weird. Once Trotter bet on a dog, that was in Florida, named Principo, and it came out of the gate peeing. Principo relieved himself for about twenty yards, then took off running, and lost the race by six inches to a dog named Flamer, which peed *AFTER* the race. This leak cost Trotter one thousand smackers, because he bet two hundred dollars on Principo, which would have paid 4–1. The difference between plus eight hundred and minus two hundred was but a tinkle. Then there was the time he bet two hundred dollars on a basketball game, the Knicks. The Knicks were at home against some patsy like the Pistons, and the Knicks were favored by eight. Pro basketball is where guys have systems. There is one guy who drives a cab, Peters is his name, who keeps charts and graphs. Peters was a very well-known football player at Sunny High, back then. He showed the guys his clipping from the paper. One day Peters hurt his foot and the local paper ran the headline:

SUNNY HIGH TO PLAY WITHOUT PETERS.

Anyway, Peters keeps results of who wins how

much, where, and why, and what the humidity was in the gym. Peters' system has proved conclusively that in pro basketball, a team will win the *SECOND* time it's home after a road trip. Peter calls this his Jet Lag Backlash Index. Guys coming home, Peters says, are pooped and don't play good the first home game, but get rested and play good the *SECOND* home game. Peters' system has proved conclusively that a pro basketball team will win its second home game, sometimes. He has got killed quite a few times with eastern teams coming home after trips like Boston to New York, which are hard to get jet lag from since they ride the bus.

Trotter didn't believe much in systems. A team like the Knicks plays a weak bunch at home like the Pistons, it doesn't take a graduate of the M.I.T. department of numbers to figure the bet. The bet was the Knicks, minus eight, meaning they had to win by nine. That time, the Knicks were up by nine with three seconds left and some idiot Piston threw one overhanded from mid-court. The basketball hit the back of the rim and bounced straight up. It bounced so high, all the players were in the shower by the time it came down. As Trotter had two hundred dollars on the re-entry, he stayed close to the TV set. The ball came down right through the center of the hoop, for Christ's sake, so the Knicks won by seven and Trotter lost the bet. Trotter handled the original picture of this event quite nicely, but the replay did him in.

"Oh gee," the ignorant woman color announcer said, "that was some bounce. I just kind of wonder what the odds are on a half-court shot like that going in, Bill? Gee, I bet 1,000–1."

During the slow motion replay of the tape, Trotter kicked his TV set in and his wife left him that night.

For a moment there in the john, the wet quarter securely in his pocket, Trotter wondered if his wife was living at home right now. She had left so frequently, he wasn't quite positive. Of course she was. He had told her he had to work today. She accused him of sneaking off to the track. He just left the apartment. She, Pam, said if he went to the track she would leave him. He, Trotter, said how could he go to the track with no money. That, Pam said, was the first logical thing he had said in two years.

"You'll probably stop along the road and pick up pop bottles and cash them in and use that money, you're *THAT* disgraceful."

That had hurt. Until he found the quarter in the pot.

Trotter remembered a few other bets he had lost that were almost occult in nature, like the time he bet a hundred dollars on Rutgers and lost on a ninety-nine-yard pass, the last play of the game, and the time he and a few guys were pitching pennies after work, twenty dollars a pitch, and Trotter's last penny rolled down a drain.

One thing was for sure, Trotter was due.

So was the Second Coming of Christ.

The only thing keeping Trotter from living up to his potential was a lack of money.

He dedicated himself to positive thought, and rejoined his table, where Sid Booten had pulled up a chair and was saying things like, "The goddamn two horse in the second is a mortal lock and I'm going to wheel him."

It was like Tweetie Bird cussing.

The only thing keeping Sid Booten from being one of the world's finest saxophone players was he had no idea how to play the saxophone. He sure *LOOKED* like a saxophone player, all thin, and he

39

SOUNDED like a saxophone player with that name, Sid Booten.

He weighed maybe a hundred and thirty, counting some jewelry that looked like it had been made by the Cleveland Indians. Sid thought the bracelets and necklaces were made by real Indians. There was a shy blonde on Sid Booten's arm and she was blinking a mile a minute, wondering what she was doing here. She looked like she should have been twirling a burning baton at half time of a high school football game. She was also thin and tipped the scales at approximately ninety, counting her eyelashes.

She wore braces. Quite a few people frequently seen in Marty's wore braces. This child wore them on her teeth.

Marty gives 3 per cent off on the drinks to guys who wear braces, old jockeys and things.

Since rules are rules, Marty decided to give the kid girl 2 per cent off her choice, which was a Shirley Temple, hold the Temple.

"What's that?" Marty asked the kid.

"Um, straight Hawaiian Punch, I think," the girl said.

"What's Hawaiian Punch?"

"I don't know."

"Is this a joke?" Marty asked Sid Booten.

"Get her a brew."

"What's that?" Marty asked.

"A beer, you know," Sid Booten said.

"Oh," Marty said. "Forgive me. Most people call beer beer."

When the beer was fetched, Sid Booten tipped Marty a buck, which impressed the blonde so much she smiled at her date, which caused Vibes Eberhart to comment, "Who the hell is her orthodontist, Ray Charles?"

The kid did have a tremendous lot of crooked wire in her mouth.

She blushed and covered her mouth with her right hand, tangling her watch in the braces.

Trotter, Looney, Vibes Eberhart, and Marty watched as Sid Booten deftly removed the watch chain with a fork.

"Boys," Sid Booten said, "meet Evangeline."

"What boys?" Trotter said.

"Evangeline is a poem," Evangeline said.

"Evangeline, meet the boys. Trotter, Looney, Vibes Eberhart, and Marty."

"Can I see your ID?" Marty asked.

Evangeline fumbled through her purse and came up with a driver's license. Marty looked at it and said, "She's nineteen." He gave her the beer. Evangeline blushed brightly.

"Nineteen?" Vibes Eberhart said. "I got a dog nineteen, for God's sake."

Sid Booten blushed.

He was dressed in a silver suit and vest, and looked like a baked potato.

"This is the first time I ever been to the track," Evangeline said. Looney watched the Giants circle the wagons by calling a time out. Vibes Eberhart rubbed his eyes because of all the smoke. Trotter looked at the *Racing Form*. "I brought my camera," Evangeline said.

"Give you three bucks for it," a bum from the next table said, which scared Evangeline, and she scooted next to her escort.

Sid Booten said, "Relax, lover."

Trotter had known Sid Booten maybe two years. He came in one day with a guy named Everett Tone, who was currently serving two to five years at the state penitentiary for stealing things. Sid Booten and

Tone were cousins, something sweet like that. Sid Booten was a real meek little character and had a Coke that day as Tone explained such things as what it meant when a horse came in first. Booten is a commercial photographer. He had never gambled before, but immediately liked the intimacy of it, the closeness that losers share, and he quickly became a regular. Losers, as a rule, are very friendly. Sid Booten is now one of the boys; Lufkin, his bookie, is a GOOD friend.

"How's the kid," Lufkin says, slapping Sid Booten's face.

Sid Booten pays dearly for membership in this fraternity, to the tune of about two hundred dollars a week. Lufkin doesn't give out inside information about how much a client is down, but he has frequently told Trotter, "You think you're in bad shape, you ought to see the kid's sheet. He couldn't pick a winner after the fact."

It doesn't seem to bother Sid Booten, though, because he has a bunch of pals and a place to go.

There are a lot of little elves like that, Trotter thought, as he watched Sid Booten wrinkle his nose at a beer. Trotter knew all about gamblers and why they gambled. Some guys, like Booten, gambled because they were shy and couldn't make friends the conventional way, like shaking hands instead of palming some bookie a hundred. Some guys gambled because they had trouble at home, or at work. Gambling, you see, is a major diversion, kind of like sex, only with gambling, you never know who's going to win. Also, with gambling, as opposed to with sex, you can make a comeback. As an extra bonus, you can do it all day.

When you have a pretty good load on a horse like at 10–1, and he's hanging in there at the top of the stretch, *NOTHING* matters, not the rent, not a headache, plus you don't have to worry about the horse getting pregnant.

Every person, Trotter learned, gambles for a serious reason.

Trotter was told that he gambled because he was self-destructive, and that he had a compulsive desire to lose, which pissed him off so much, he bet the guy who had said it a hundred dollars. He offered to take a lie detector test to prove losing was the *LAST* thing in the world he wanted, that he wanted more than anything to win. Everybody made noises through their teeth and shook their heads at Trotter like he was some sort of maniac.

"Screw 'em," Trotter said.

"Right, screw 'em," Sid Booten said. "Who, though?"

Evangeline blushed.

Trotter said he was just thinking out loud.

"The Packers just scored," Looney said. "A guy ran a sixty-yard quarterback sneak, fumbled on the one, and the center recovered in the end zone. It's 17–0. I'm fucked."

Evangeline blushed.

Sid Booten explained to his date that fucked when used in connection with a bet meant "in trouble" and not anything dirty, right, boys? He then bought a popcorn popper from Hugh Sipe for four dollars. Hugh Sipe had two teeth, fortunately one above the other, so he could chew a little. High Sipe, who said he knew Hitler, went to third grade with Minnie Mimosa, and escaped from San Quentin twice, said the popcorn popper was worth at least ten bucks.

"Who is Minnie Mimosa?" Looney asked.

"Only one of the famousest baseball players there was," Hugh Sipe said around his teeth. "And I went to third grade with the bum. Went on to play with the cocksucker of a White Sox, that's who."

Evangeline blushed for a long time.

"You remember him," Trotter, who was getting very depressed, said. "They named a tree after him."

"Oh," Looney said.

"You goddamn right," Hugh Sipe said.

Sid Booten handed the good as new, one-owner popcorn popper that had been removed from the trunk of an old Plymouth, one of those trunks where if the button is sticking out, that means the trunk is unlocked, to Evangeline, who frowned at it, then put it under her chair.

"He knew Hitler," Looney said to Evangeline of Hugh Sipe.

"What a cocksucker," Hugh Sipe said.

"Oh," Evangeline said.

Hugh Sipe then tried to sell a coat to Evangeline that had belonged to his ex-wife.

"The reason she is ex," Trotter told the girl, "is because she is dead."

"Hey," Hugh Sipe said defensively. "She didn't die *in* the coat. I swear to God, it was in the closet."

Evangeline excused herself to use the ladies' room, which was also the men's room, and she opened the door on some guy in there shaving. She about fainted.

Marty got Hugh Sipe by the nape of his neck and led him to the door.

Somebody at the bar was nursing a beer, loudly. The guy stuck a thermometer in the beer and said it had a fever. The drink, he yelled, was 87 degrees.

"Take it or leave it," Marty said.

The guy nursed it a while longer, but it died anyhow.

Trotter was suddenly weary of this place. He

didn't belong here. He should be over in the Jockey Club talking to guys with all their teeth, rubbing knees with ladies wearing see-through blouses, getting tips from owners.

Life is a whore.

You need cash to play.

Some of Trotter's past suddenly popped into his mind.

It took one minute to capture the highlights.

After junior college, he was offered a tryout with a major league baseball team, and the first morning he struck out twenty-two consecutive times. Some goddamn hillbilly was out there throwing howitzers. He joined the police force and was a cop six months until some dope addict shot Trotter in the foot. The police *LOVED* guys with junior college. To become a cop, Trotter had to answer correctly such questions as, "Would you ever shoot an old lady in a wheel chair for jaywalking?" After quitting the police, he signed up with the cab company. The cab company *LOVED* ex-cops. That was eight years ago. Oh yeah, somewhere in there he had married Pam.

Driving a cab was a better job than one might expect because there was a shield between the driver and the rest of the population, which is about the best deal a person could hope for. When Trotter saw the shield, he signed up to be a cab driver on the spot. Lawyers don't have shields keeping the fruitcakes off. Doctors don't. Cops sure the hell don't. It's great, very secure and private.

"What's wrong?" Looney asked.

"You get a vibe?" Vibes Eberhart wondered.

"My life just passed in front of my eyes."

"Christ," Looney said. "Maybe you're having a heart attack."

"What'd it look like?" Vibes wondered again.

Trotter said he was just thinking of when he was a cop.

Vibes Eberhart nodded and looked at the racing program. "Trotter, you just had a minor vibe on the horse Counterfeit. Cops, Counterfeit. It goes together."

"What's a vibe?" Evangeline asked.

Sid Booten and Vibes Eberhart explained the process. Trotter grabbed Looney by the shoulder and nodded toward the door. The Giants were taking gas to the tune of 17−2 late in the second quarter.

"I have to win fifty-five dollars in the first race to start even," Looney said, "which is impossible."

Marty yelled at Trotter to remember Blurred Image, and he switched the *HAPPY HOUR* sign on.

HAPPY HOUR: NOON UNTIL 12:45.

"Inflation," Marty said.

LOONEY BOUGHT A TIP SHEET FROM SOLLY FRIEDMAN, which surprised even Solly Friedman. Hardly anybody who knew Solly Friedman bought one of his tip sheets for the simple reason they were rotten.

Solly Friedman's name is Jim Reynolds, at least it was until he tried selling tip sheets as Big Jim.

The first day he tried that, he sold three and his wife bought one, but returned it after the second race and demanded her money back. The other two people who bought Jim Reynolds' tip sheet the first day he was in business thought they were buying *LITTLE* Jim's tip sheet, and as Big Jim told them, all sales are final, take a leap.

The first day Jim Reynolds sold tip sheets, the horse he picked in the first race finished ninth and the horse he picked in the second race finished seventh. His Daily Double couldn't have outrun Huey and Louie, but what's remarkable is that even though he sold only two copies of *Big Jim's Poop Sheet*, and even though his horses in the Daily Double finished next to last and third from last, he broke even. He had printed a hundred copies for a total cost of four dollars, and since he sold the sheet for two dollars, hell, it played.

As great as breaking even can be at the track, Jim Reynolds did a little market research and came up with a way to clean up. He changed everything. The only thing that has remained the same since he went in business pushing tip sheets two years ago is his skill at picking winners.

He has none.

Jim (Solly) Reynolds (Friedman) was standing in front of Marty's yelling, "Had the Daily Double," and Looney coughed up three dollars for a copy of the *Kosher Nag*, the new name of the sheet, since *Big Jim's Poop Sheet* didn't take off so hot.

Jim (Solly) Reynolds (Friedman) was holding up his tip sheet with his thumb over something important so you couldn't see. Looney was suckered by the claim of "Had the Daily Double."

The thumb was over the date when that particular Daily Double was hit, which was sixteen months ago. Furthermore, the Daily Double that day paid fifteen dollars.

"Hey, sue me," Solly Friedman said when Trotter told Looney he had been suckered. Then Solly Friedman recognized Trotter and Looney and said, "Oh. Hi." He wondered why Looney bought the sheet.

"You said you had the Daily Double," Looney said.

"All sales are final," Solly Friedman said.

Jim Reynolds changed his name to Solly Friedman the day he bought all the tip sheets sold in front of this track, and checked the names out. There were nineteen tip sheets, with titles like *Big Jim's*, *Little*

Jim's, *Big Al's*, *Little Al's*, *Fat Bob's*, *Skinny Bob's*, but there were no flagrantly Jewish tip sheets. The next racing day, Jim Reynolds did a survey in front of the main gate and determined that 39 per cent of those in attendance were Jewish to a certain degree, originally, or by marriage.

The day after that he changed his name to Solly Friedman.

The day after that he started cleaning up.

He sells one hundred tip sheets priced at three dollars each at seven race tracks a day. That's $2,100 a day, minus a $70 printing cost or, approximately $2,030 as the crow flies.

The crow flies first class.

The seven tracks where Solly Friedman circulates his bullshit have a total of seven hundred racing days a year, so two grand a day times seven hundred is $1,400,00 a year, isn't it.

"I know," Solly Friedman said, reading Trotter's lips. "It's a lot of money. What can I say?"

Solly Friedman pays the guys who sell his sheet 10 per cent, which means Solly only clears a million, two, a year, printing picks that hardly ever win.

"Looney, for Christ's sake, here, take your three bucks back," Solly said. Solly Friedman gave Looney the *Kosher Nag* on the house.

"You don't *REALLY* like Chiquita's Banana in the first?"

"Never heard of her," Solly said.

"But you picked her on the sheet."

"You're so ignorant, I'm *TAKING* your three dollars," Solly Friedman said, and he did so.

TROTTER EXPLAINED TO LOONEY THAT NONE OF THE people putting out tip sheets knew beans about

48

horses, so that was why they were putting out tip sheets instead of selling shoes. Trotter asked Looney please not to act like some hick that just fell off the bus.

Trotter wished severely that he had come alone to the track, but after all, Looney gave Trotter Charity in the first. He owed Looney *some* company.

Trotter had never received a tip like the one Looney gave him on Charity. He never dreamed such a thing was possible.

"It does not look bad," Looney said as they listened to the tape on the way to the track earlier this morning, "but the horse will probably swallow its tongue or something."

They had agreed to bet the hundred dollars they won at Lufkin's right on Charity's hot little nose.

"Hot nose?" Looney had said. "That means she's sick."

Trotter planned to lose Looney in the crowd after the first race.

Trotter had to hear the tape one more time. It was forty-five minutes to post time. He told Looney he would meet him at the paddock, by Charity's stall. He gave Looney the fifty dollars he had coming and told him to put it under his tongue and not let some midget who claimed to be a doctor have a look.

Jake was still parking cars.

The Buick was on the front row.

Jake was off to the back of the lot, so Trotter used the extra set of keys and got in the front seat. He took the tape out of the glove box and played it.

Don't tell anybody, but the shield in cabs isn't really bulletproof. It's foolproof, though, because a person with a gun isn't going to fire a bullet at something with a little "Bulletproof" sign in the corner.

The cab company was faced with the problem of spending something like 7 trillion dollars on bulletproof shields or something like $11.95 on adhesive "Bulletproof" stickers. After the executive board met, it was decided by a vote of 11−1 (one member had an uncle who made bulletproof shields) to go with the little stickers.

It was not a popular decision with the drivers. Cabs are natural targets for the lunatic fringe, and people like dope addicts were knocking over an average of twenty cabs a day. Drivers were getting shot at like the front seat was a shooting gallery.

So the company put in plastic shields, which cost roughly one twentieth the cost of bulletproof shields (one board member wanted to go with cardboard), and "Bulletproof" stickers.

The shields are soundproof.

The board said that if many more drivers were murdered, they would re-evaluate their position concerning the shields and stickers.

The plastic worked.

The reason they worked was the drivers didn't know they weren't bulletproof at first. The first week the plastic shields were in, a driver named Pierce picked up a fare at about Seventy-second on the west side. This neighborhood is very unique and oozes with character. If you're not careful, though, your character could ooze out onto the sidewalk. Beautiful old apartment houses and sleazy dumps are brick-to-brick. Pierce picked up a guy and said, "Where to?" through the little mouth-hole in the shield.

The guy pulled a pistol and screamed, "Gimme your cash."

Pierce quickly closed the speaking slot.

The guy screamed, "Gimme the cash or I'll blow your head off."

Pierce couldn't hear the guy.

Since Pierce thought the shield was bulletproof, he put his thumbs in his ears and wiggled his fingers at the lunatic who was wielding a pistol in the back seat. Pierce drove from the curb with the guy going crazy in the back. The guy put the pistol right *ON* the shield and considered pulling the trigger, at Pierce's neck. Pierce was still making funny faces and driving. Pierce had one of the newer cabs with a switch under the glove box that closes and locks the back doors, so a lunatic can't get out. Pierce was playing the radio, having a hell of a fine time. The guy in the back was going berserk. He read the "Bulletproof" sticker in red print, and the danger warning underneath it, which said anybody shooting a bullet into the bulletproof shield did so at his own risk. Management was not responsible for lost eyes, ears, or throats. Some of the drivers working the neighborhoods where English was what you put on a cue ball were a little worried because the foreign criminals and dope addicts might not understand "Bulletproof," so the company put up stickers in eleven languages, and even a drawing with an X through a bullet for those who couldn't read.

The guy with Pierce decided not to blast away at the shield and Pierce drove around a few minutes until he found a beat cop. Pierce got out and explained the situation, which was he had one dope addict with a pistol back there. The cop signed the voucher and the city paid Pierce the fare, and there is one less dope addict to worry about, leaving only about a hundred million.

You do your part, you know?

A driver's gun accidentally went off and the

shield shattered, and the company admitted it was true, the shields were only kind of bulletproof. But the company brought out charts and graphs proving that the plastic shields at least diverted the true course of a bullet, which reduced the odds on a driver's being hit from 98 per cent (without the shield) to 51 per cent (with the plastic shield).

The hell with that, the drivers decided.

There were threats of strikes.

The company said that if one driver got killed, the plastic shields would go and the bulletproof shields would be installed, plus the drivers got a bigger share of the take in a new contract.

The drivers thought the proposal over and decided more money was worth the risk of being shot at and the 51 per cent risk of being hit and the 22 per cent risk of, if you were shot at and hit, being snuffed.

Since the plastic shields, not a driver had been killed.

In a cab.

The usual amount were terminated in bars by wives.

Trotter had been robbed four times and in each instance he happily handed the cash over to the dope addict. The company had an insurance policy for pilfered funds and Trotter always jacked it up a few bucks.

When they put the kind of bulletproof and mostly soundproof shields in, Looney rigged up a microphone under the back seat hooked to a tape recorder under the front seat, and since the fares didn't think the drivers could hear, they said some entertaining things back there under the guise of privacy.

Very dirty, very crooked, very weird, and very interesting.

It was like a confessional. Looney sat up front and pretended he wasn't interested, just like a priest.

Looney got the goods last Thursday. Trotter took the tape out of the glove box of HIS Buick in the lot across from the track and ran it through to the good part. He couldn't help but listen quickly to some of the more *entertaining* highlights.

"Hey, cab man, you hear me?"

"He ain't hearin' nobody, man."

"Hey, white man. You so ugly, cab driver, you so rotten ugly, so *MISERABLE* ugly, I got a mind to twist that ugly head around so when you pass somebody on the damn street, they won't be sick."

"He ain't hearin', man. The thing don't let no sound through."

"Thump, thump, thump."

"Quit thumpin' on the shield, man. You piss him off."

"Ugly white man. I'm pissin' in the back seat."

"Man, he's smilin'. He ain't hearin' nothing."

"Okay, okay."

"Damn, Julius. You got to calm down, man."

Looney had the microphone in his ear. Everybody thought he was listening to a ball game or something.

"You know what to do?"

"Damn, Julius."

"You got the gun, right?"

"Damn!"

"You take the goddamn gun and put it down the man's throat and I get the goddamn money."

"Damn, Julius, man. *I KNOW!*"

"You *GOT* the goddamn gun?"

"Oh, *MAN!* I got the gun. I got the guts. And I got the need!"

"Now, Ronnie."

"What."

"Don't be takin' whiskey like the last time. You luggin' five quarts of whiskey, man, you too slow."

"Okay, Julius."

"Okay, Ronnie."

During the latter part of this conversation, Ronnie and Julius decided what to do if the man who had the gun down his throat didn't like it:

"Damn, man!"

"Hell."

"Hell, man, damn!"

"Aw, man."

"Damn."

"Damn nothin'."

"Hell, man."

"You *WHAT*?"

"I what, nothin', man."

"Hell."

"Damn!"

"He won't do *NOTHIN'*, man."

"I hope."

Looney had called the dispatcher and was patched through to the liquor store owner at the address given by the passengers. Cops were called. Julius and Ronnie were pinched. Looney was given a twenty-dollar reward by the liquor store owner.

Julius and Ronnie didn't know exactly where they had gone wrong.

Trotter ran the tape ahead and listened to a conversation involving a man who wanted to take his secretary to the Holiday Inn but she didn't want to go because her husband had a knife and was very jealous. The man said he was going to leave his wife and the secretary said in that case, she *WOULD* go to the Holiday Inn, so that's where Looney took them. The woman refused, however, to wear a pillow case over her head during sexual intercourse. She said that was

54

demeaning and proved the man didn't really love her. He asked if he could at least take pictures and she said that was also demeaning. He could, she said, call his wife during sexual intercourse if it was absolutely *necessary*.

Trotter got to the important tape.

Looney picked up a fare last Thursday at a nice hotel and was told to drive to a bank, where another man was waiting. He drove these two guys around the park.

"Can the driver hear?"

"Ask him."

"Can you hear me?"

"He can't."

"I need some money."

"Who doesn't."

"I need some right now."

"Who doesn't."

"I want to borrow five thousand bucks."

"Why?"

"I got a horse running Saturday that looks good. It's running in a cheap claimer with some cripples. The horse hasn't won in eight times this meet and the odds will be jacked up pretty good. We've held it back all year."

"What do you mean?"

"I mean we've held it back. Kept it from winning."

"You mean it could have won, but you kept it from winning to get the odds up next time out?"

"Yeah."

"Is that legal?"

"Long as nobody knows. Odds of 15– or 20–1 pay more than a couple of wins at 2–1. It's simple. We got a crop of dogs Saturday. My horse will win. We're letting her go, flat out, wire to wire."

"I thought there was no sure thing in racing."

"There isn't, for the tourists."

"You want five thousand dollars to bet on the horse?"

"Right."

"What do I get?"

"This tip. Bet on the horse yourself. I'll pay you the five thousand back Monday morning."

"What if it loses?"

"It won't."

"What collateral? I can't give you a signature loan for that."

"The horse."

"What's it worth?"

"Five, six grand."

"Those the papers?"

"Yeah."

Looney said there was much shuffling and little conversation for a few blocks.

"You say this Charity is going to win going off at what odds?"

"Fifteen, ten, twelve."

"Tell you what."

"What?"

"I'll loan you the five thousand myself."

"Okay."

"No bank. No interest. No collateral. I'll draw up the papers this afternoon. Five grand against the horse. I want the money back Saturday night."

"Done."

"There IS one thing."

"What?"

"The horse better not lose."

"She won't."

"If she does, I want an extra two thousand. That's what I'll bet at the track. You owe me the five-thousand loan Saturday night. Charity wins, that's it. She loses, I want my two thousand covered. That's fair."

"Done."

"Stop back by in two hours."

"Appreciate it, Dad."

Trotter put the tape back in the glove box.

Looney, in his infinite ignorance, hadn't paid much attention to the tape. Trotter heard it accidentally. It was sandwiched in between the Holiday Inn episode and one where a guy tried to get his brother's wife to get in a bathtub full of beer.

When Trotter heard the trainer telling the banker-father the fix was on, he told Looney something like this came along an average of once every four lifetimes.

The way Looney's luck had been running, which was in place, he figured those guys were two actors or something rehearsing.

Trotter had slapped Looney.

"You, jackass," he had said, after hearing the tape a thirteenth time, "this is the most important thing that ever happened to either one of us."

"It is?"

Trotter had sighed hopelessly.

"It's a shame we don't have any money then," Looney concluded.

Well, they had hustled the hundred from Lufkin's. That was a sign from God if there ever was one. Sitting in the front seat, Trotter felt different. He couldn't explain it.

Maybe the way he felt—kind of silly—meant he was on a hot streak. He had never been on a hot streak, and didn't know how to feel.

Maybe, on the other hand, he had swallowed a little chipped glass or plastic. That might explain the weird feeling in his stomach, also.

One thing he knew for sure, being around Looney made a person think twice before blundering into a good mood.

Lufkin called him Approximately Looney because he had not had a winning week in approximately three years.

Trotter replaced the tape and got out of HIS Buick.

"It's great to be alive," he said to a couple of women laden with tip sheets, binoculars, *Racing Forms*, and sacks of food.

"Why?" the skinny one said.

The question caught Trotter off guard.

The women walked away.

"Hey, I got a guy for you to meet," Trotter shouted. "He's at the paddock. You'll love him. You two can talk about what would happen if the roof caves in."

THE PADDOCK IS WHERE THE HORSES AND PEOPLE ARE saddled.

The horses are saddled with saddles and the people are saddled with the responsibility of picking a winner from among twelve horses, or, in the case of the first race here, twelve *alleged* horses.

The nine horse, Neutron Nelly, looked like a big donkey.

The one horse, Myrtle's Delite, was trying to scratch its stomach with its back leg.

The three horse, Shy Ruler, had blown its cheeks full of air.

The four horse, Klass, looked like it had a stiff neck. Its head was tilted sideways.

The five horse, Blurred Image, Marty's hot flash, was biting at flies.

The six horse, Chiquita's Banana, had started foaming at the mouth ever so slightly.

The seven horse, Dream Roadblock, appeared to be sleeping.

The eight horse, Fancy Sparrow, was yawning.

The ten horse, Counterfeit, was full of lumps like two guys were inside it.

The eleven horse, Lo Fat, was watching ants.

The twelve horse, Guys N Dolls, was reading his trainer's *Racing Form*.

The two horse, Charity, was Trotter's.

He stood on his toes but could only see the top of Charity's ears; they looked all right. He yelled for Looney, who yelled back "Up here."

Looney had secured a spot at the rail of the paddock.

There are those, experts and amateurs alike, who believe that valuable information can be secured from close observation of the horses at the paddock.

It happens.

Once Trotter had a horse in mind and as he observed it in the paddock, it suddenly fell to its side and threw up.

Trotter took the ten dollars he had been planning to bet on this animal and bought a roast beef sandwich and beer and watched happily as this creature finished sixth.

Unfortunately, what you see, or *think* you see, at the paddock, isn't worth a damn, nine times out of eight.

Trotter has had some dehumanizing experiences at the paddock.

Once he saw a horse snapping its jaws and pawing the ground and chomping at the bit. He bet twenty dollars on this good attitude and lost. Another time, he observed a horse beating its head on the stall. The horse was terribly lathered. Trotter took the ten dollars he had planned to bet on that nervous wreck and bought a roast beef and beer. The horse won and paid thirty bucks.

Generally, the paddock is for the widows who think the color of a horse's skin has something to do with how fast it moves its feet.

Solly Friedman, in one of his surveys, determined that 99.4 per cent of the Jewish women frequenting this race track thought gray horses ran faster. Solly Friedman *ALWAYS* puts the grays in the money. Jewish women, they don't particularly care if you're right, as long as you agree with them.

The only reason Trotter would be caught dead at the paddock was because he wanted Looney to have a look at Charity's trainer to see if it was the same person on the tape.

"*IT'S HIM, TROTTER, IT'S HIM,*" Looney screamed.

Trotter closed his eyes and begged Looney to be quiet.

Charity was still conscious, even bordering on alert.

The horses to the right and left made, in Trotter's opinion, Charity look almost good.

The one horse, Myrtle's Delite, was still trying to get at the itch on its stomach.

The three horse, Shy Ruler, seemed to be giggling to itself.

The way it works in the paddock is the trainer, owner, and jockey hang around. The horse is saddled. The jockey gets a let up, then in about fifteen minutes, there is a race.

"Hey, Myrtle," somebody down by the first stall said, "your horse has got fleas."

Fat Myrtle sniffed.

A guy to Trotter's right was making a prophetic statement about a horse's ass in relation to its won-loss record. The gist was, a big ass makes a horse a winner in the long race. The first race was a mile, seventy yards. Medium long.

"The four horse [Klass] has got the kind of ass it's going to take to win this race," the guy said to his date, who nodded. "You take a horse with a large ass in a field like this, you got a winner, just like with women."

There are as many theories about what a horse should look like as there are theories about why girls go out with jerks like the one to Trotter's right. The guy told his date the next important thing was the size of a horse's forehead. "You get a big ass and a small forehead, you go to the bank."

"The blood bank," Trotter said. "To sell some blood."

"What?" the guy said.

"Nothing," Trotter said.

"He said something gross to you, Bobby, I almost heard it," the girl said. That explained her. She also was a jerk. She had a gold tooth in front.

"And just who do you like?" the guy snarled.

"He likes the two horse," Looney leaned across and said. "Charity."

Trotter thanked Looney for shooting his mouth off. Trotter was a little jumpy.

"The *TWO* horse?" the guy said. He looked quickly at his *Racing Form*. "That one couldn't outrun the dog catcher. Christ, it's got leprosy."

Trotter asked the guy what he was doing wearing a shoelace around his neck.

"It's a string tie," the guy said.

"He's being gross again, Bobby. Slug him out."

Bobby and his gold-plated date went to bet Klass, with a capital K.

"You make your bet?" Trotter asked Looney.

"Her coat *IS* a little rough-looking," Looney said of Charity.

Trotter said that the only thing keeping Looney from being a little old lady was he only had fifty dollars.

With people, Looney said, when your skin looks bad, that means you're sick.

"What the hell do you think this is," Trotter said, getting a little more irritated, "the Olympics? You think the damn trainers are going to run a foot race? What are you talking to people for? This is a horse race!"

A little old woman to Trotter's left applauded politely.

"I like Charity too," she said. "He's got a cute nose."

Looney said he hadn't made his bet yet.

Charity's jockey was named York.

York stood at the front of the second stall, rubbing Charity's nose.

The trainer, the one Looney heard borrow five grand, was standing next to Charity's owner, a woman, according to the program, named Betty Flannigan. The trainer was smiling, Betty Flannigan was smiling.

"It's in the bag," Trotter told Looney, who shrugged.

The trainer put the saddle on Charity, and the horse's ears flicked.

Another popular misconception about the racing racket is what famous last words are spoken before the jockey hops on the horse.

Most people think the owner says something like,

"Here's the plan. Stay wide around the first turn. Move to fourth at the top of the backstretch. Cut inside the three horse at the half-mile pole. Rate her real good. Swing wide at the top of the last turn. Snap back to the rail and whip her with your left hand, two whips every eight seconds."

That's crap.

It's more like what a football coach says to his team before the kickoff, which is "Kill somebody" or what a manager says to a pitcher who can't find the plate, which is "Are you nuts?"

Back in the days when Trotter frequented the track a whole lot, he knew a few jockeys, one named Mikey Malone. Mikey said the advice he most always got from the owner or trainer was:

Please win the goddamn race.

Or, if the owner or trainer had bet a wad on somebody else.

Please lose the goddamn race.

Mikey told Trotter quite a few of the races were as crooked as the track.

Trotter told Mikey, so? They might fix one in his, Trotter's, favor.

Mikey told Trotter he ought to see a doctor.

Sometimes Mikey *KNEW* who would win a race, but *STILL* wouldn't bet.

He saw a horse drop dead once.

Looney's!

Mikey said each race was different and each horse behaved differently each time out, particularly in lousy races, so strategy was meaningless.

Trotter read Charity's trainer's lips as he told jockey York:

"Go fast and win the goddamn race."

"Going over important strategy," Looney guessed.

Other owners told other jockeys such in-depth things as:

Stay on the horse.

Go fast.

Win the goddamn race.

The next time you're at the paddock looking for a secret message just between the horse and you, and the owner goes over and puts his hand on the jockey's shoulder, you'll be able to amaze your friends by telling them exactly what they're talking about.

Charity had opened at 20–1 in the Morning Line.

Trotter checked the odds board above the paddock. Charity was down to 12–1.

The trainer's five grand about cut the number in half.

"I'm going to bet," Trotter told Looney. "You want me to make yours?"

"You *REALLY* think she's going to win?"

Trotter again explained the importance of the information they had. It was the next best thing to a conversation with the Heavenly Father. Trotter explained that he had fifty dollars in his pocket and approximately nineteen dollars in the bank. He was going to turn around and walk to the fifty-dollar window and purchase a win ticket on Charity. Yes, he thought Charity would win. What did he have to do, cut off an ear?

Looney mentioned several other times he and Trotter had marched confidently to the fifty-dollar window, only to bet a loser.

"I got a feeling Charity will lose by a nose," Looney said.

Looney saw the world through cumulonimbus-colored glasses. He had lost so much and so long, his mind was distorted.

Trotter pushed his way from the paddock.

The widows from New Rochelle were out in force, and they had made Counterfeit, a gray, the favorite at 5–2. Counterfeit was the one that looked like it should be in burlesque, the one with lumps instead of curves.

Trotter looked up at the odds board again.

Charity ticked up to 13–1.

Thirteen times fifty is six hundred and fifty dollars.

That's a lot of money.

Trotter had to walk around the paddock to get to the betting windows. The people hanging over the rail on the far side of the paddock—where such prizes as Fancy Sparrow, Lo Fat, Dream Roadblock, and Guys N Dolls were displayed—seemed to be a little drunk-looking.

One guy was slumped across the rail, right next to Counterfeit's stall.

Is what you get for standing too close to those lovelies, Trotter thought. You get sick.

A guy looking at Lo Fat shook his head, as if to clear it. You get dizzy sniffing the glue in those stalls.

The horses were called to the track for the first race, the first half of the Daily Double.

They used a bugle to call the horses.

Should have used a dog whistle, Trotter thought.

TONY CHEESEBURGER WAS LEANING AGAINST THE wall by the fifty-dollar window, checking things out. He pretended to read the *Racing Form*. He pretended to have fifty dollars to bet when the mood hit him.

All kinds of people hang around the fifty-dollar window, the high rent district. There are high-hitters picking their teeth with twenties, women in mink, and creeps leaning up against the wall eavesdropping. Quite a few tourists hang around the fifty-dollar window to absorb a little color.

Trotter got in line behind a little guy with a roll of lettuce that would choke a horse. The most Trotter ever bet on a horse was four hundred dollars, six months ago, and it choked the horse, all right. The horse choked so bad, it almost *backed* across the finish line, fifth, the gutless, choking wonder. That day, six months ago, was the last time Trotter had been to the track. It was the last time he had gambled. Right after that, he went in for the Cure.

"Well, well, well," Tony Cheeseburger said when he recognized Trotter. "What are you doing in that line, some aunt die?"

"Taking a survey," Trotter said.

Tony Cheeseburger used to work for Lufkin, but was fired when Lufkin decided a name like Tony Cheeseburger was not conducive to the bookie business. It looked bad, having a guy working for you named Tony Cheeseburger, arrested once a week. Lufkin is a pioneer in the movement to get the guys to change their names from things like Pizza Face Mancanelli to Al Mancanelli, and Nutcracker Bocabella to John, and Tremendous Louie Spinoli to Lou.

"The guys are like kids," Lufkin told Trotter once. "They think the nicknames add to their prestige."

You have to admit, Nutcracker Bocabella has a ring to it.

Tony Cheeseburger looked like he was wearing Sammy Davis, Jr., around his neck. His shirt was open to the waist, exposing pendants, necklaces, and other cheap crap.

"Am in the import and export business," Tony Cheeseburger said to Trotter. "Kind of."

"Heard you opened a funeral home," Trotter said.

"That's it. It's a living."

"For dogs."

"Hey. Them little things has got feelings too."

After Lufkin fired him, Tony Cheeseburger got on driving a cab, but he wouldn't go by his regular name there, either. Retired ladies and gentlemen from Duluth didn't feel secure looking at the picture and name *TONY CHEESEBURGER* on the sun visor.

"Who do you like?" Tony asked Trotter, who was trying to pretend he didn't know the bum.

"The two horse," he said quietly.

"You're kidding! That's no horse. That's a joke. Nobody in his right mind bets the two horse. You must not think much of the aunt that died and left you the fifty bucks to bet it on a crumb like that."

Tony Cheeseburger went on like that for another minute, and Trotter summoned a member of the track security force. "Get this bum out of here," Trotter said. "He's bothering the customers."

"Bet or move on," the guard said.

"Hey everybody, that guy's betting the two horse."

Several big-hitters looked at Trotter, and he flushed slightly.

"Is that funny or not, betting the two horse?"

Tony Cheeseburger was dragged away from the fifty-dollar window. His jewelry rattled like a wind chime.

TROTTER HAD GONE IN FOR THE CURE FOUR MONTHS ago at the urging of his wife, who said she could no longer live with a person who was insane.

If you love me, you'll do it, Pam had said. As extra-added incentive, she said she would take the car, the furniture, and every penny Trotter had, and would ever have.

That, the pennies, didn't worry him. It was the

car and the furniture he had grown accustomed to.

"You can live at the Y," Pam said. "I'm keeping the apartment."

He signed up.

The organization was called Gamblers Limited and you went once a week. You had punch and cookies and exchanged horror stories.

He met all kinds of people.

He learned why people gambled.

He heard lectures from psychiatrists and mathematicians and he learned that habitual gamblers were losers. Of the sixty-five members of this chapter, not a single person had won money gambling over the long run.

The fourth week, he got up and said, "My name is Trotter and I am a loser," and he was rewarded with a smattering of applause.

Pam was very happy.

Things were going great. The first few months Trotter was off gambling, he saved maybe five hundred bucks.

Then he was robbed.

Each gambler received semi-private counseling in groups of four. Trotter was something of a landmark case. Most habitual gamblers gambled for a very specific reason. Trotter gambled for *ALL* the reasons.

He was not satisfied with his job, thought he was overqualified, and gambling provided the opportunity, theoretically, to get the money he deserved. His marriage was less than stable. He enjoyed gambling. He continued to gamble despite the loss of many thousands of dollars. When all this was put before Trotter in the group session, he had to agree, he was a little nuts.

It was proved by one of the guest speakers, the

mathematician from Harvard, that it was impossible for a habitual gambler to make money. That was depressing. This guy had done a doctoral thesis on gambling and gamblers. He had studied the case histories of two thousand habitual gamblers, guys and women who gambled regularly, at least each weekend, and only three people won money over a three-year period. And those three won lotteries or contests. One guy won four grand on a lottery and pissed away all but thirteen dollars of it betting football in sixth months.

A man named Love ran the Gamblers Limited sessions.

He had gambled away more wives and money than Trotter had ever thought about.

Addictive gambling, Trotter learned, is different from other illnesses because unless you lose and are unable to settle up and get your arms broken, you don't go through any physical torture, with the possible exception of starvation.

It isn't like alcohol addiction, or drug addiction, where you climb the wall.

Withdrawal from gambling doesn't hurt at all.

That's why it's so hard to quit.

It's like quitting smoking after a good lung X-ray.

It's only a pain in the figurative ass.

The secret, Love said, is everybody has to stick together. All of those who think you gamble to make money, kindly sit down with your bank statements and determine how much you've lost over the years.

There are many reasons for quitting gambling, Love said.

Anybody who is remotely fond of money *has* to quit.

What you miss is the action.

Action is fun.

Jay Cronley

That's why they had Action Night. It was Freddie Star's idea, and a lot of guys blamed him, but he had a decent alibi—the three hundred dollars he lost. It was probably Lufkin, since most of the members used to gamble with him, and a dozen or so were really big spenders.

Action Night was scheduled because of what one of the psychiatrists called the Vice-Versa Syndrome, which was the substitution of another habit, or vice, to replace gambling.

Some personal good came from the desire to fill the spare time vacated by gambling. Approximately 80 per cent of the men who gave up gambling started chasing women. One of the guys, Abe Munson, chased twenty-nine women, he said, the first Saturday he didn't bet on football. He tackled one girl in the park, even. When Abe compared notes with the others, and found that his symptom was not that unique, he dropped out of Gamblers Limited and opened a place called Women Anonymous, which he plans to franchise. This organization gives counseling to guys who run around on their wives. After hanging out his shingle, Abe had a hundred and three customers the first week. He's thinking about branching out into a Men Anonymous in the near future. What started out as a noble idea has since changed. Instead of trying to get the men to *stop* running around on their wives, Abe and his counselors are giving them advice on how to get away with it.

Women Anonymous is a big hit. Abe has three stores already, at $13.95 per head, per week.

That's a lot of money.

Anyway, quite a few of the people at Gamblers Limited expressed the opinion to Mr. Love, who had a scar on his forehead where a bookie threw him through some plate glass, that whereas everybody understood gambling was rotten, and whereas it was a disease, and whereas it was destructive, and whereas it was a blatant escape from reality, and whereas everybody felt better and got along better at home and at work since quitting, whereas all that, you just can't go cold turkey from the *ACTION*.

There *HAD* to be a way a person could get a little action. It was a need you couldn't ignore. Some of the people had been gambling twenty years. A call to one of the counselors at three in the morning didn't do much good.

Freddie Star came up with his bonanza of an idea, Action Night, where the main room of Gamblers Limited would be converted into a casino. There would be a crap table, blackjack tables, and a roulette wheel. Members could bring REAL cash and gamble their guts out, but no more than three hundred dollars. Any member who won money could keep 10 per cent of it. Any member who lost money would get back 90 per cent of it. The remainder would go to the house for improvements.

This would satisfy a person's *need*, without subjecting him to financial ruin. It would be a healthy jolt to Gamblers Limited's pocketbook.

OH, PLEASE, MR. LOVE, everybody said one night. *PLEASE!*

Mr. Love decided it would be a fine idea. The games would be different from some of those found in Las Vegas. They would be totally honest. The house would get only its God-given mathematical cut, like with double zero on the wheel. Mr. Love concluded that it would be a graphic example of how, *even* under ideal circumstances, you can't win.

The masses sang he's a hell of a jolly fine fellow.

Casino Night, Action Night, was three weeks ago Friday.

71

Upon entering the front door, Trotter was a bit queasy. He had had some unpleasant experiences in Las Vegas, like the time he played blackjack all night and then threw up on the table. He had found some crooked games in the sleazy joints where, for a nice tip, a dealer would give you the shirt off his back, a good card, anything. They cheat in the dumps.

You bet ten dollars or twenty dollars at blackjack, and tip five dollars, they let you win. Sometimes they let you win and win. Since hardly anybody who has been winning and drinking all night can quit, they send in the sharpie about dawn. You keep thinking, the dealer's just making it look good for the others at the table who aren't tipping big. You're up about five hundred. You bet a couple of hundred, with a twenty-five-dollar tip, and lose a couple of those, then you throw up on the felt.

The big houses don't need to cheat.

At the dumps, they cheat. If you tip big and can quit when you're a couple of hundred ahead, you can win money in the dumps, where the dealers look like winos, and their hands shake.

You can win money *once*.

The secret is to hit the dumps, tip big, and quit each place when you're a hundred ahead.

That's hard.

You keep thinking, maybe they'll give you cards all night. Maybe the woman dealer, she loves you!

She doesn't. They'll give you the five- and ten-buck pots and get you three-quarters drunk, then they'll get everything back.

It's a popular misconception all the games in Las Vegas are fair, since the built-in house advantage should be enough. A crooked blackjack dealer in one of the dumps can play a single deck of cards the way somebody good plays the piano. They can stack decks, deal seconds, and make a face card change expression.

In one dump Trotter used to hit, the dealers would say things like, "Be nice to him," meaning Trotter, when the dealers changed shifts. This meant Trotter tipped good. This meant let him win a couple of hundred, get him drunk, and then while he's sitting there grinning, gut him.

The reason they cheat in the dumps is to get the big money out. Get you ahead, and you think, hell, this is easy. In the fancy places, the big money is always out. In the holes, they charm it out by letting you win and taking your tips, then, of course, they hair-lip you.

So *THEY* get the tips and the house gets the money.

At an up-and-up place, the house gets the money. Wonderful.

Trotter played blackjack at Action Night.

Various members of Gamblers Limited volunteered to deal and work for the house. They wanted to be on the other side, for a change.

A guy named Lewis Wrigley hit eight on the roulette wheel the first time out, but twenty-five minutes later, he was down one of his three hundred.

Trotter played blackjack between a man named Benji Black and a woman named Liz Ashback, who confessed at one of the counseling sessions she used to sell narcotics to kids in junior high to support her gambling habit.

A member named Gus Wintergarten was the dealer at Trotter's table.

Gus dealt the first hand, looked at his cards, and said, "I'm good, I'll stay."

"Hell, you're the *dealer*," Liz Ashback said.

Gus said, "Oh, yeah, that's right. I wondered why I had a hand of twenty."

It was very busy and very successful the first hour.

Since all the members had brought three hundred dollars, all their wives and husbands were caling to make sure they were *REALLY* there, and not off whoring around somewhere.

Trotter started off the way he usually did, playing blackjack, winning a little. Gus Wintergarten was having a lot of fun playing dealer, flipping the cards around like a pro.

Love circulated throughout the room with his hands behind his back, like a father who was proud his children were behaving.

A few of the "house" volunteers had trouble with the rules, but all in all, the evening got off to a very fun start. At the end of an hour, Trotter was up forty-five dollars.

A guy named Julie Blackstock played one hand of blackjack for three hundred dollars, and hit twelve with a face card, and proclaimed the evening a ridiculous waste of time.

Trotter had his forty-five dollars in winnings stacked neatly in front of him when a man wearing a brown sack over his head with a rubber band around' the neck and eyeholes cut out entered the front door with a request. His request was that nobody move. His seemingly outrageous request was made more practical by a shotgun, which he carried.

Three more crooks wearing similar sacks entered and closed off the exits. Women screamed. Men swore. Sacks were filled with money.

In the neighborhood of twenty-one thousand dollars was stolen from the members of Gamblers Limited.

One of the crooks shot a wad of shotgun matter into the roof, then they left. Nobody moved.

The members decided that a person could have had a lot more fun with three hundred dollars than giving it to crooks. Even betting it on the Giants would have made more sense.

Love rose to the podium and made an impassioned speech about how this bit of bad luck was merely a test of the members' will power. A couple of people heard him as they left.

"Be strong, people," Love screamed.

Trotter heard there were nine people at the next meeting.

After the robbery, Love put his arm around Trotter's shoulder and said that because of the progress that had been made, it would be a shame to fall back into previous routines.

"You were a loser," Love said.

Trotter thought of the lessons he had learned at Gamblers Limited as he stepped up to the fifty-dollar window. He remembered what it felt like when the man wearing a paper sack on his head took Trotter's $345, watch, ring, and sunglasses.

It had been boring as hell.

"Give me a win on number two," he said.

He removed the fifty-dollar bill from the waistband of his shorts.

The ticket seller quickly glanced to his left at a program to check the name of the two horse, then he said, "Sir, this is the fifty-dollar window. The five-dollar window is to your south."

Trotter said he knew where he was and what he wanted. He wanted a fifty-dollar win ticket on the second horse, Charity.

The seller frowned and gave Trotter one last chance to come to his senses, to reconsider.

When Trotter said nothing, the seller hit the proper button and a ticket shot up.

"Thanks," Trotter said.

"Believe me, it's nothing," the seller answered.

TROTTER BULLIED HIS WAY OUTSIDE AND TO A SPOT ON the rail at the finish line, where Looney stood chewing his fingernails.

Trotter gave a man named Simpson five dollars, and Simpson pushed the entire row of spectators down the rail. There must have been five hundred people along the rail. Simpson is a brute of a man who makes a living clearing good viewing space for guys with five dollars to spare. He assumes a position at the finish line one hour before the first race.

He makes about twenty, twenty-five bucks a race, which is a lot of money. That's about two hundred and forty dollars a day, a grand, four hundred a week, for being big.

Not bad.

"Thanks, Simpson," Trotter said, handing Simpson his fiver.

The bodies along the rail were still rippling two hundred yards up the track from Simpson's mighty shove.

"You got it," Simpson said. "Who you like?"

"That one," Trotter said, pointing at Charity.

"One thing's for sure," Simpson said, squinting. "It hasn't got a coat. It's got a *JACKET*."

Trotter started to say something about judging a book by its cover, but decided to save his energy. Simpson used to park cars in a lot on the other side of the track but was fired for rolling a Toyota.

"Down in front, you big lug," somebody from the rear shouted.

Simpson turned slowly and asked, "Who said that?"

Nobody had said that.

Simpson was about six-eight. His head was the size of a basketball.

"Where you been, Trotter?"

"Well."

"Well what?"

"I've *BEEN* well."

"Oh," Simpson said, wrinkling his enormous forehead. It looked like a washboard. "I get it, I think. You've been well."

"Now I'm sick again."

"Oh. You want I should get a doctor or something?"

The horses approached the starting gate.

"There's nothing wrong with me a win couldn't cure."

"Oh."

"I've got a bad feeling," Looney said for the thousandth time.

Trotter asked him how he could possibly know that. To have a bad feeling, one had to have had a frame of reference, a GOOD feeling.

It was a neat day, cool and clear. The air was crisp, and it almost invigorated a couple of horses. Somebody had obviously told Blurred Image it was Marty's forty-star. Its head hung low, like it was suicidal.

The horses gathered behind the gate in a line.

Trotter was paged. At least he *thought* he was paged. Simpson hadn't heard it. Looney thought he heard it. It sounded like, "There is an emergency call for Mr. J. Trotter."

What made the page unlikely was that nobody knew Trotter was at the track.

"Probably only a mirage," Simpson said.

Trotter recognized quite a few of the faces along the trail. A man named Crawford was five or six bodies past the finish line. He and Trotter exchanged pleasantries and admitted as to how it was great to be alive again. Crawford clutched two handfuls of ten-dollar win tickets. His face was contorted into a sinister smile. He looked almost hysterical. Trotter had met Crawford at Gamblers Limited. The robbery had been too much for poor Crawford. He also had fallen off the wagon, but he came up firing.

There was color in his cheeks.

The horses went into the starting gate without a major incident. The eight horse, Fancy Sparrow, thought she was checking into the Hyatt Regency and about nodded off.

The gates flew open, ka-whomp, and twelve thoroughbreds thundered up the track, with a few minor exceptions.

The twelve horse, Guys N Dolls, tap-danced up the track, doing a few jokes.

The seven horse, Dream Roadblock, looked around before coming out of the gate, like her slip was showing.

Those few hundred dopes who had cash on her at 20–1 moaned hopelessly.

Simpson grabbed the rail and shook it and the earth trembled.

Charity broke fast like the champion she wasn't, and she went by the grandstand like it was standing still, which was quite an accomplishment for a horse in the first race. Buyers for dog food companies scratched Charity from their notebooks and drooled over and put stars by the seven horse, Dream Roadblock, who finally summoned up the courage to leave the gate. She plodded onward like a Clydesdale.

At the first of four turns, Charity was up by four lengths.

Jockey York was high in the saddle with things well in hand.

Behind Charity, the horses were bunched. About four of them were shoulder to shoulder like a drill team.

Trotter's heart went at it like a jackhammer.

Charity had burst forth at odds of 13−1.

Run away with it, wire to wire, the guy on the tape had said.

Looney said, "There is a long way to go."

"One more word, and I'll kill you," Trotter said to him.

"Well fuck," Looney mumbled. "It's a free country."

The rail at the finish line is an emotional place. Trotter had been there one Saturday with a guy named Roebuck, who had a bundle on a horse that lost by a bottom lip. Roebuck went berserk. He hurdled the rail and ran down and up a little cement drainage ditch, and jumped the second rail, the one that keeps the horses from wandering into the crowd, and vice versa. Roebuck ran onto the track and waited for his losing horse and jockey to trot back. He suddenly grabbed the jockey and wrestled him to the ground and slugged him out for riding a stinking race. Security guards eventually swarmed Roebuck and dragged him off, and a clear photograph of that appeared on the sports page of the *Times*, above the cutline: FAN RUNS AMOK AT TRACK. Roebuck's wife didn't care for the picture, since Roebuck was supposed to have been out of town on business. They threw him in jail for a couple of days and banned him from the track.

Roebuck was a dozen or so bodies left of Trotter

today, wearing a fake beard, but anybody looking closely would have noticed those crazy eyes.

Trotter remained as calm as possible as the horses made the first turn and straightened out for the backstretch.

When the field, all except Dream Roadblock, who was trailing along like a tin can, went behind the tote board in the infield, Trotter checked the column where the leaders are listed. Charity came out the other end of the tote board leading by, unbelievably, *EIGHT* lengths.

There is no feeling that rivals having fifty dollars on a 13–1 shot that is eight, no nine, lengths in front with a half-mile to go. The only feeling that comes close, Trotter guessed, was a blind hog finding an acorn.

Such a monumental event as birth even paled in comparison.

Crawford was leaning over the rail, looking up the track, screaming, "Come on, you bastard," at his choice, even though the horses were fillies.

Looney was calm.

Roebuck down the way had ripped off his fake beard and was yanking at his hair.

People were very vulnerable in the heat of combat.

More pockets were picked when the horses hit the top of the stretch than at any other time.

Trotter's win ticket was securely crunched in his right fist.

For another five dollars, Simpson would pick a person up for an even better view. Trotter was okay, leaning over the rail.

Here they came, like the cavalry.

Trotter squinted up the track.

You have no depth perception, looking straight

onto the horses. Charity came out of the final turn first, and in about two seconds, the other horses appeared. The race announcer said it was Charity by ten lengths. Trotter saw another horse swing wide to pass.

"Eight lengths," the announcer said. "Seven."

Blurred Image was the one on the outside, trying to be a pest.

The horses seemed to get no nearer the finish line. Were they running on a treadmill? Blurred Image kept wide.

Trotter promised God he would quit smoking, drinking, and swearing if only Charity could win. He would become a missionary and walk to India to help the poor children.

ANYTHING!

"She's dying," Looney said matter-of-factly.

Trotter backhanded Looney in the neck without looking.

Then he kicked him in the shins.

A race, by God, is a slice of life. It's condensed, of course, but you do the best you can and you win or you lose. Why screw around with the cop department, getting shot at by dope fiends? They don't pay you 13 – 1 if you live, for God's sake. Betting on a horse isn't that much different from investing in the stock market. You win or you lose. There's no wait. Trotter bought some stock once. The President of this country got a sinus headache and the stock went down four points. It cost six dollars a share. Races make more sense than THAT.

Charity's jockey, York, began whipping the animal, casually at first, and then to beat the band.

Charity was on the rail.

Blurred Image veered in from the outside.

Charity had clearly run out of muscle and was finishing the race on guts.

Blurred Image was making up ground by the second, and with about twenty yards to go, Charity was but a length in front.

The rest of the creatures were far back, bumping and grinding for show money.

When it became apparent the race would go down to the wire, Trotter planned on keeping his eyes right down the finish line since he was *on* it, so he could see who won. That's hard to do, though. Instead, he watched the approach of both horses, Charity on the inside, real close to the rail, being whipped to a froth by jockey York; Blurred Image not a foot from Charity, feeling her oats.

Charity leaned and Blurred lunged and the horses crossed the wire.

The cheering stopped.

Those by the rail were frozen in a vacuum, mouths open, eyes unblinking.

The whomping of the horses' hoofs echoed in Trotter's ears.

It was a couple of seconds before the third-place horse lumbered by.

Trotter felt himself sinking into shock. He couldn't move his arms or legs.

"Who won?" he said weakly.

"Was close," Simpson said.

Crawford up the way said he didn't give a damn who won and he flung his losing tickets in the drainage ditch.

Roebuck threw his fake beard in the ditch.

The people who had neither Charity nor Blurred Image wandered off to prepare their guesses for the second race.

Trotter and half a dozen other guys remained at the rail.

"The horse on the outside was coming hard," Simpson said. "You never know."

Charity and Blurred Image trotted back toward the winner's circle, both thinking they had won. Charity was exhausted. Her trainer was there. He was white as a sheet.

"It's a good thing I decided not to bet it," Looney said. "I would have had a heart attack."

Trotter gave Looney a murderous look, and Looney backed off.

Charity's trainer and jockey exchanged comments. The jockey shrugged. The trainer shook his head.

Trotter stood there a few seconds, watching the tote board for the official winner. It was like waiting for news of which lucky soldier got to carry the flag and lead the troops up the beach. Trotter threw his cigarettes and half a pint of hooch into the drainage ditch as confirmation of how serious he was about winning this race.

The tote board flashed:

PHOTO.

TROTTER GAZED NERVOUSLY AT THE RUMPLED PACK OF discarded cigarettes in the cement gutter. He wanted one bad. He wanted to jump the rail, place the whole package in his mouth, and light up and suck the smoke down into his toes.

He wanted smokes, whiskey, and women.

Since a deal was a deal, though, and he had made his pact with the Great Steward in the Press Box in the Sky, Trotter put his hands in his pockets and pawed the blacktop like, of all things, a horse.

Jay Cronley

A photo finish is where the race is too close to call with your eyes, so the judges meticulously study the taped replay of the race. This tape is then relayed to various televisions throughout the stadium so everybody will know for sure they weren't skinned.

It was nice to know the film would be studied on the up and up and that the real winner would be announced.

Some places, it didn't happen that way.

Some places, you got the winner from the horse's mouth, the horses were that high.

Trotter had earned his spurs, that was what you bet sometimes, at the dirt tracks in places like Texas, Oklahoma, and Kansas. Trotter was born in Dallas, three light-years ago, it seemed, and his father worked for a company that liked to keep moving, liked to keep one step ahead of the Better Business Bureau. Trotter's old man sold things, many of which the company he worked for really owned.

His father was a man who had the sporting spirit, and since horse racing was not legal in places like Texas, Kansas, and Oklahoma, what the sporting gentleman did was go to a dirt track for a little action.

Trotter went, too.

Some places, they check your age.

At the dirt tracks, if you *HAD* an age, you got in for a buck.

A dirt track is a place where all races, creeds, colors, and sizes of horses ran. Races were made up on the spot. When one owner said to another owner, "Screw you," that usually meant a race had been made.

The tracks were dirt. So was the infield. So was everything.

A dirt track where money was bet was illegal, but so was pissing into the wind in public. The sheriff never got too mad unless he bet on a horse and they ran in a ringer. Sometimes the horse that ran in a race was not the horse that was listed on the program, which was illegal, immoral, and hard to tell, since the owners frequently painted over distinguishing characteristics on horses.

A horse could sweat his spots off.

Some horses wore sweaters or blankets to cover the needlemarks.

There was no track physician on duty to see that a horse had not been doped. Doping was not a particular advantage at a dirt track because *ALL* the horses were doped. Some horses came onto the track full speed. Trotter remembered one horse that was named W.C. Fields, it had the shakes that bad.

Names didn't mean much.

You took the black one or the brown one or the one with a sore on its side. Most of the races at dirt tracks were match races, two horses. The tracks were so rough, you got more than two horses running at the same time, the jockeys flew all over the place.

Most of the jockeys were named Junior and were the sons of the owners of the horse.

The only facility at most of the dirt tracks was a beer stand where fiery brands like Shiner beer were sold. Shiner is a native Texas beer brewed in Shiner, Texas, in a plant the size of a good sneeze. Whatever else can be said about Shiner, like it could melt the shell off an armadillo, one thing was for sure: you could get it cold. Shiner was made by hand, although some swore it was made by foot. Six of those babies and you couldn't tell one end of a horse from the other.

He lost the first hundred dollars he ever made at a dirt track near Houston.

At the dirt tracks around there, guys let excess air

out of the tires of their Lincolns with hundred-dollar bills. Some guys made airplanes out of hundreds and sailed them to the whore section of the grandstand. Still other guys used hundreds for fans.

Trotter learned at an early age Houston was wicked.

There is a lot of oil money there and those old boys like to let everybody know how the cow ate the cabbage, and this was done by carrying and betting enormous sums of hard cash.

Nobody ever tried to rob a dirt track. He would have been shot 135 times. Everybody carried a gun.

It was the lack of adequate technical equipment that cost Trotter his first hundred-dollar calamity. He was seventeen.

There is no tote board at a dirt track. There is no nothing. The way you make a bet is to say, "Hundred on the black one," and somebody else would say, "You're on," or "Your ass," and that was that.

Now, the trouble was, a sizable portion of the audience at a dirt track is black, or rich and potbellied. A kid could make a dozen different bets and forget who the hell owed. Trotter's father taught his son at an early age to bet only with people with unusual characteristics if you didn't know the guy or the track, bet guys with limps, with one eye, one ear, like that. Each person had his "territory" at a dirt track. If he won a bet, he would go to that "territory," like by the water fountain, and the losers would limp or crawl or hiccup by and settle up.

Some guys who lost would just as soon you forgot them. Some guys *FAKED* limps, and after they lost, walked like they had just met Oral Roberts on the backstretch. You couldn't suddenly pop in an eye, so that was who Trotter made his first bet with, a rich, potbellied guy with a glass eye.

Trotter took the brown one, Black Joe, for a hundred.

The other guy took the black one, Bob.

The race was a mile, once around.

It was so hot that day, you had to duck when the sun went over. Trotter had had three Shiners and was feeling no pain, pulse, or hair.

Horses at a dirt track don't come out of the gate. They come out of nowhere. They stand around and some guy shoots a gun and the fun begins.

Trotter's horse, Black Joe, was so doped up, it didn't hear the gun, and got a bad start.

Bob took off like a bat out of hell.

It was hard to follow them on the backstretch. Cars and trucks were parked on the infield, where pavement grew up through the grass. When it was about 115 degrees, you saw mirages across the infield. The temperature seldom rose to 115 at midday. It usually FELL to it.

Trotter's horse, Black Joe, made up some ground on the backstretch. Trotter prayed to God Black Joe was sober enough to turn for home, and not sail through the fence. Both horses were ridden by Juniors, sons of the owners.

There was no weight allowance for this particular race. Sometimes they had "live weight" races, which meant all you had to have on a horse's back was something "live," something like a chicken. It was mildly entertaining to have a hundred on a horse carrying a rooster on its back. There were many ways to bet. You could bet "daylight," which meant your horse had to win so there was "daylight" at the finish, more than a length. You could bet "moonlight," where your horse had to finish by dusk.

This was a straight hundred, winner take it.

87

"Come on, Black Joe," Trotter remembered yelling.

He was watching the race next to an old duster, which is the dirt equivalent of an old salt. The old boy had seen it all. The whore section came alive. Being a whore at a dirt track was a lot like being a bookie. You couldn't lose. A winner every time, like you say at the fair.

"That ain't no goddamn Black Joe," the old boy next to Trotter said.

Despite the heat, Shiner, and screeching from the whore section, Trotter heard that.

"It isn't?" he asked.

"Goddamn no, son. The goddamn Black Joe has got a white spot on its butt. You see that on that there one?"

"Thought," Trotter said.

"It was pure-D shoe goddamn polish."

"Oh no," Trotter said. His heart sank below C-note level.

"But that ain't old Bob running against him, neither."

"What?"

"That's a goddamn ringer brought down from Oklahoma, name of Jude. I seen him before. Bob has got a broke foot or something."

Trotter asked the old boy who the hell WAS running out there?

"A black one and a brown one."

Black Joe, Trotter's horse, which was neither black NOR Black Joe, made up more ground. It was somebody's neck and somebody's neck at the top of the stretch.

Everybody went to the rail and looked up the track.

The wind was blowing from the south, so the

dust arrived before the horses and about smothered everybody as the horses blasted past the finish line. Trotter's jockey, Junior, had ridden an interesting but fairly effective race. He had beaten the horse all the way around the track, like he was riding his grandpa's back.

"Well, that's a damn photo if there ever was one," a woman shouted from the shack. Her name was Lucy and she worked the camera. The shack was suspended near the finish line, up some stairs. Sometimes when a race was close, they ran it again. The horses didn't care for that. Some died. This race was one-shot, take a picture if it's close.

Lucy had a Land camera that made a picture quick. Her brother watched the horses and said "Now!" when they hit the finish line, which was a wire stretched from the shack to a post.

The judge's decision was final. Lucy and her brother carried shotguns. Once a sore loser tried to fry the shack.

While waiting for the quickie picture of the photo finish to develop, young Trotter wandered onto the track and lined up the finishing wire with the photo shack. The wind had been blowing so hard of late, it had blown the shack so it pointed about three feet farther north than the finish line!

The goddamn photo was of a point a yard *PAST* the official finish!

Trotter decided not to protest, however, when the photo proved that Bob or whoever the hell it was had won the mile and one yard race by a nose. He paid the hundred dollars he owed without comment. Trotter was firmly convinced his horse had won it by a fraction at the real wire, but as they say at the dirt track, "Screw you," meaning another race had been made.

You can't cry over spilled beer.

Trotter inhaled another Shiner and fifteen seconds later forgot he had probably been clipped.

The dirt track was an education.

Trotter learned to subtract there.

Thank God for instant replays.

You could roast hot dogs on the stairs leading up to the photo shack when Lucy FORGOT film.

IT'S HARD TO BELIEVE THAT TWO HORSES CAN RUN A mile and seventy yards and be nose-to-nose at the finish line, which isn't even a line, it's a speck. It's so hard to believe, Trotter almost threw up to prove it, but instead, he sat down on the concrete with his back against the rail.

"That's why I only bet two bucks a race on the longest shot there is," Simpson said, counting the money he had made clearing space at the rail the first race. "So my heart won't get broke. You take the craziest one there is and then if you come real close, the only thing that gets broke is your fist when you smash it."

Simpson asked which horse it was again Trotter had?

"Two," he said.

"A real shame," Simpson said. "Hey, wait a minute. Two's in the photo. You still got a shot!"

It was also hard for Trotter to believe that Marty's horse, Blurred Image, was a potential winner. The presence of one of Marty's picks in a photo finish was grounds for a free beer with the purchase of five. A winner would bring the house down. Blurred Image's color picture would replace Citation's over the bar. When Marty hit Citation in 1948, he was so overjoyed, he bought a round for the house, a round of cheese bits, but it was the thought that counted.

It was ironic. It was as though Marty, personally, beat Trotter. It was like losing a debate to a guy who had had a lobotomy.

"You know what's hard," Simpson said, "is picking LOSERS. There's this guy named Jackson that's here a lot and one day he was going on two hours about how unlucky he is, right? This Jackson, he says he can pick every loser there is, in his sleep, anywhere. Well, I listen awhile and then say, Jackson, you're so bad, you can't even pick a loser good. Now the way you get bets, Trotter, is you insult the man, get personal, piss him off. Jackson says, oh yes I can. I say, oh no you can't. I say, I got twenty-five dollars that says you can't pick the loser of the next race. Jackson, his eyes light up and he says make it fifty dollars. Suit yourself, I say. Why not make it two hundred dollars if you want to suit somebody. Make it two hundred dollars, Jackson, you can suit me, buy me a new suit, get it? Anyhow, Jackson goes over the *Form* trying to pick the last-place horse. There are about six on death's doorstep, right? Now, it stands to reason it's as hard to pick the last-place one as the first-place one, right? It is. I used to make four, five grand a year when I was parking cars at Santa Anita doing the pick-a-loser routine with all the big shots. See, the leaders are trying to win. You got two or three or four of those. You got nine others back there trying to sneak across the line without the relatives recognizing them. So Jackson comes up with this horrible thing named Skim Skam that looked like it ought to be used for putting kids on for fifty-cent snapshots. You could have played a tune on its ribs. When you got a bet on the loser, Trotter, it's a little different race to watch. Here's me and Jackson at the wire. The winners go by and everybody wanders off, but there's me and Jackson, screaming like hell. People thought we were nuts, Trotter. Slow down, you bastard! Jackson is going. Slow down! Five minutes after the winner, here comes Skim Skam, way back. Jackson screams, I did it. Pay me! Excuse me, Jackson, I say, then I point up the track. Here comes this thing named Lucifer the jockey had eased. I swear to God, it was walking! By the time it finished, Jackson's Skim Skam was in taking a shower. Jackson about faints, but hits me with four crisp Grants, right? The track ought to figure a way for a guy to bet losers, hell, they'd clean up. Make a thing up where you try and pick the last two horses of the first two races. Call it the Daily Crapper, who knows?"

"What?" Trotter said.

The PHOTO sign had been on several minutes. That's a long time. Maybe they forgot film, like Lucy.

The last time Trotter felt like this was when the dentist was reading the X-rays of his wisdom teeth. That was a fun wait.

After a few minutes, the dentist looked from the X-ray to Trotter and said, "You know, don't you."

"Yes, I know," Trotter had said.

So much for the wisdom teeth. Four of them were pried out like stumps from a field; similar equipment was used for each job.

Another time Trotter had a wait that didn't have a good feel to it was just before the dope addict got cute. Trotter cornered this guy in an alley. The dope fiend had a pistol, which he turned on himself. The kid weighed about a hundred and twenty pounds, a couple of which were bags under his eyes.

Scenes of this nature are seldom seen on the police-recruiting posters.

Trotter peeked around the corner, according to the book, and said what he was supposed to say, something like, "Come out with your hands up," or, "Throw down your weapon," or, "Son, what would your mother think if she saw you now?"

The way you peek, by the book, is you crouch down. Guys with guns assume you will peek at eye-level, so if you crouch, you'll trick them.

Trotter crouched and peeked.

The kid had the pistol right at his own temple. "One more step and I'm going to blow my brains out," the kid yelled.

Trotter started to yell back, "What brains?" but he didn't.

Instead, he unpeeked and considered his next move. By the book, he seemed to remember, his next move was to call the dispatcher and go have a cheeseburger. Several people from apartment buildings had seen him, however, so he decided to hang around. He called for assistance.

God, he thought, the gold stars were piling up.

For some reason, Trotter decided during the wait, while the kid was shaking and holding the pistol in a suicidal position, to pretend he was on "Dragnet" and arrest the entire goddamn city single-handedly, beginning with this punk.

Trotter pitched his gun into the alley and stepped out.

He said, "I'm not going to hurt you," to the kid.

"That does it," the kid shouted. "I'm going to kill myself."

"Oh hell," Trotter thought.

"No I'm not," the kid quickly reconsidered.

The kid ducked and pulled the trigger and the bullet ricocheted off the alley wall and struck Trotter in the right calf, which hurt like hell. Furthermore, the dope fiend escaped by stepping over Trotter and stealing his police car. Trotter's partner was guarding the back way against things like Martian attack, and missed the whole fiasco. Trotter was able to save face by making up a story about a gun battle, then he quit.

That ricochet, one of the detectives said, was about a 500–1 shot.

Trotter should have felt better about Charity at 13–1.

Plus he wasn't shot.

Pam had said quitting the police department was the coward's way.

Looney saw Trotter sitting there, leaning up against the rail with his head in his hand like a wino, and felt sorry for the guy. He had bought Trotter a beer. He put it at his feet. He was a little worried Trotter might turn on him like a mad dog, so he stayed back.

Looney felt great about not betting the race.

"You all right, Trotter?"

"Sure," he said.

"Here's a beer."

Trotter informed Looney that he had quit drinking. At that moment, the crowd, which was impatient with the delay, hushed.

"Trotter!" Looney said. "The PHOTO sign's off. They got a winner."

When the winning number was flashed in the box next to 1st on the tote board, about four people in the stands cheered. The rest went, "Ah, horseshit."

"My God," Looney said.

He bent over and shook Trotter by the shoulders. "You won! Charity won. It's official. You won!"

Trotter looked up into Looney's eyes, which were the size of binoculars. Looney knew better than to tamper with Trotter's emotions at such a critical stage in each man's life. Looney gave Trotter an elbow up, and Trotter scrambled to his feet, leaning on the rail.

He quickly looked at the tote board and saw 2 by the box reserved for the winner.

Trotter opened his right fist and saw the fifty-dollar win ticket with the 2 on it.

Presently, the winning money was put on the board beside Charity's number:

$28.40.

That's what Charity paid on a two-dollar win ticket.

Looney figured what a fifty-dollar win ticket would pay, and announced it was $710. "My God, Trotter, you're rich. I can't believe it. You won."

"I won? It's official?"

"Yeah."

"How much?"

"Seven hundred and ten dollars. I can't believe I didn't bet it." Looney removed his fifty dollars and gave it a sad look.

"You're a fool is why," Trotter said.

The "OFFICIAL" light WAS on. Sometimes there was a protest by a jockey, and they changed the winners. But this one was over, official, all of it.

The owner and trainer and jockey were having their pictures taken with Charity. Trotter loved those people. The trainer was jumping up and down with pleasure.

"It all evens out," Looney said philosophically. "I'll tell you one thing. I'd hate to walk around this place with seven hundred in cash."

"Seven ten," Trotter corrected him. "You will never have to worry about that problem, Looney. The reason I won is because you didn't bet. You're worse than Marty. You're the unluckiest person in the world."

"No I'm not."

Trotter was letting it go to his head, Looney thought.

"They call you Approximately Looney because you haven't won a bet in approximately five years."

"I have so."

"When?"

"It's none of your business. Who calls me Approximately Looney?"

"Everybody."

"Well that's chickenshit."

"It's the truth."

"There's no need to get personal."

"Who do you like in the second?" Trotter asked.

"I don't know. I guess the six horse. Not bad."

Trotter took the program from his back pocket and marked a heavy line through the six horse. Marty had earlier given him the two horse. "Only six horses left to worry about now," Trotter said.

"That's rude," Looney said.

"Got a brother?"

"In Cleveland," Looney said. "Why?"

"Call him and ask him who HE likes. I figure it's in your blood."

Simpson asked Looney how he was doing.

"Two bucks behind," Looney said, looking at his beer. "Not bad for not having bet yet."

"Me neither," Simpson said. "But I'm thirty dollars up."

Trotter was paged again, for SURE. Emergency call for Mr. J. Trotter. Manager's office.

"Hell with it," Trotter said. "I'm busy."

"Why?"

"I won. I've got to collect."

"Oh yeah, but I still can't believe it," Looney said.

Just between God and Trotter, he couldn't either.

"Pages scare me," Looney said. "Usually it means somebody died."

Trotter smiled. He said he doubted it.

Looney wondered why?

"I just doubt it. It could be a GOOD page. Maybe I won a car or something."

"I still bet somebody died."

"How much?" Trotter asked.

ONE OF THE MANY THINGS TROTTER HAD FAILED TO consider, in addition to the serious likelihood of victory, was: what in the hell does a person do when he wins a lot of money? Where does he carry it? Trotter hadn't brought a billfold to the track in many years.

Seven hundred dollars and change is a *lot* of money.

He found it funny considering ten dollars "change." Moments earlier, he would have considered it a nice "roll."

There was little business at the fifty-dollar cashier. One guy was in line. He had bet fifty dollars to show on the horse that came in third, and was rewarded with twenty bucks.

The guy was a little nervous, collecting such a paltry sum at a ritzy window.

"Beats losing," Trotter said, consoling the guy.

There had been times when Trotter would have considered a 20-dollar win a major victory, times like the last time he bet before this.

Massive victory changes a person's outlook, even makes him slightly wittier.

Trotter placed his winning ticket on the counter. The cashier picked it up. The ticket was in poor shape, all wrinkled. The cashier asked Trotter where he found it.

97

"Oh, I didn't find it," Trotter said calmly. "I bought it. I just like to keep my tickets in a safe place, so they won't be stolen. Want me to tell you where?"

The cashier frowned and dropped the ticket to the counter.

"It's where the sun doesn't shine, unless you stand on your head, nude."

The cashier added what was due Trotter, $710

Trotter counted the money three times.

"Night school was good to you," he said. He tipped the cashier a quarter.

The cashier had given Trotter twenties. That's thirty-five twenties. Trotter was used to money you could wad and conceal in elastic. Thirty-five twenties was about an inch of stiff cash. The cashier was out of hundred-dollars bills, so Trotter agreed to take anything.

After receiving his winnings, he looked around for somebody who might consider robbery simpler than picking winners. There ARE people like that in this world, people who hang around the pay-off windows and then follow you to your car and bonk you on the head and rob you, which is the only advantage of losing:

You got your health.

Trotter put the cash in his right front pocket, which didn't work at all. The casual robber would immediately recognize the long, flat bulge as thirty-five twenties, and Trotter would be blackjacked on the spot.

He thought a moment, and retired to the rest room, but nobody was getting much rest. The guy working the towels had an open cigar box next to him. After relieving yourself, Rudy would smartly hand you a paper towel for which you were supposed to drop in twenty dollars, but Rudy would also take a quarter. He would also take a dime. Trotter had seen Rudy crawling around on all fours for an errantly pitched nickel. Pennies, though, were trash. Rudy wouldn't take pennies for handing you a towel, except five pennies.

Many first-, and quite a few second-, and a good number of third-time visitors to the track and this rest room probably thought Rudy was employed by this place, that he was paid a salary for handing out towels and keeping loose change off the floor so nobody would slip on a quarter and fall and start suing. Not Rudy. Those who came to this place regularly were aware that Rudy was a free-lancer who quickly closed up his cigar box when a track security guard arrived. Sometimes Rudy paid a kid a buck to thump the door so he could get his box closed. The track security guards merely thought Rudy had lost control of himself and had to take lots of leaks.

It's amazing how many people pay a guy to hand them a towel, a guy who is just hanging around.

Again, it's the superstition of the track.

You take a leak, and hit Rudy with a half, and win the next race, well, you do the same thing again, right? And again and again and again.

Rudy and his dancing cigar box made as much as $30 a day, $180 a week, $720 a month.

There was a time in Trotter's life, which was approximately fourteen minutes ago, when Trotter would have looked at Rudy and figured what he made handing out towels. Trotter would have thought to himself, "That's a lot of money."

Well, it's not.

Seven a month towel-handling is not BAD money, but it's not a LOT. Hell, Trotter had more than that in his right front pocket, which Rudy stared at and said, "My, my."

"Don't make a move, Rudy, or I'll snap your neck like a twig."

"My, my. I would do something about the condition of your drawers before I took too many more steps, Mr. Trotter, because unless these old eyes mistake me, I would say you got company in the form of many Andrew Jacksons."

Rudy handed a towel to a guy and received a dime and said, "Thanks for the dime. Didn't know they were still making them." The guy felt guilty and flicked in a quarter. Rudy said, "That's better. I got kids in college. They thank you. Good luck."

Trotter gave Rudy a nickel and took a paper towel and held it in front of his pocket and he quickly retired to a stall.

"What's this?" Rudy asked, holding the nickel up to the light. "Foreign money?"

Many men regarded the stalls in the john as something like the Twilight Zone. It's kind of neutral territory. You overhear guys saying all kinds of things, Trotter guessed, because it's semi-private and nobody can see your face.

Trotter locked the door and took the cash from his pocket.

To the left, he heard, boom, boom, boom. The left wall of the stall shook. Boom, boom.

"Oh, my God." Boom. "I can't believe it." Boom. "God DAMN it." BOOM. "Oh hell."

Some guy was beating his head on the wall because of what had happened, or HADN'T happened, in the first race.

"Hey, knock it off in there," Trotter said.

Some change rolled into Trotter's booth from the left. "Oh hell," the guy said. "That's my last money."

Trotter picked it up, rolled it in a one-dollar bill,

and slid it beneath the wall. The guy was quiet a moment, then said quietly, "Bless you."

"Yeah, sure," Trotter said.

The guy said, "No, I mean it. It DOES mean something, I'm a preacher."

As Trotter had said earlier, there's one of every kind at the track.

A guy in the stall to the right asked Trotter who he liked in the second, as if they were on a bus, not in booths in the john, and Trotter said he didn't know.

Various other declarations of dependence, like "God help me," came from up and down the way.

Trotter took the cash and flipped through it like it was a deck of playing cards.

"God bless everybody," the alleged preacher said, and a door slammed.

It's a shame nothing means as much as money, Trotter thought, checking his body for a place to hide seven hundred bucks. He decided on his shoes. He removed each loafer and placed seventeen twenties in the left shoe, and the rest in the other. It's a shame he couldn't feel as good as he did right now when he was poor. He wiggled his toes on top of the money. The fit was snug, but all right.

He exited the stall feeling fine.

Rudy handed Trotter a towel, which Trotter wiped his hands with.

Rudy carefully studied Trotter. "Not bad," he said.

"Good," Trotter said.

"Once a guy came in with a similar bulge and he came out of the stall grinning like a jerk. Well, there is a big crowd, and somebody knocks the guy down, and his wig comes off and tens fly all over the john, floating around like leaves. You ever see a john at a track where there are tens floating around?"

"No," Trotter said. He pulled his hair to show Rudy it was standard equipment.

"What happens is men go crazy. Men dive face-first onto the concrete. Men hit other men. It was so bad, that time, people outside heard what was going on, even WOMEN came in the men's john to go for the tens."

Trotter placed a dollar in Rudy's cigar box. "Buy yourself a new joke."

"I got kids in college. This dollar will pay for four seconds of tuition. Thanks."

Somebody thumped the door. Rudy slammed shut his cigar box and said to Trotter, "It's a crime what's going on in Russia."

A track security guard told Rudy he ought to get his bladder checked.

"I like it in here," Rudy said. "There's pickpockets and rapists and criminals out there."

Trotter pushed the door open, patted Rudy's accomplice on his filthy little head, and walked briskly for a beer.

There was no doubt about it.

Trotter had happy feet.

ANOTHER INTERESTING THING ABOUT A RACE TRACK IS: news travels faster than greased lightning.

As Trotter walked toward the stand where he regularly bought beer, for a dollar a cup, but you got to keep the cup, he noticed a figure in the background, matching him step for step. Trotter paused to scratch his ankle and recognized Tony Cheeseburger.

It is common practice for guys who lose to have a beer bought them by an acquaintance who won. A lot of guys about die of thirst around here.

Tony hung back.

Trotter waved to him.

Tony casually read one of the medallions hanging around his neck.

At the beer bar, the regulars were bitching about death, imprisonment, and the pursuit of unhappiness, and they were all trying to figure the second in the *Form*. They all regarded Trotter with scorn, like he had violated some sacred pact by winning one.

"You look a little taller," Vibes Eberhart said. His psychic vibration had finished next to last in the first race.

Trotter made a point not to look at his feet. The boys looked like vultures.

Sid Booten was explaining to Evangeline why the head was the best part of a beer. It contained the vitamins and minerals. He had tried to pay for his and Evangeline's sandwich and beer with a Texaco credit card. The beer man had to ask. "Are you serious?"

Looney was sulking in the shadows, evidently angry at Trotter for having made the bet anybody in his right mind would have forgotten. Looney didn't have a big chunk of money, but at least he had the peace of mind that comes with knowing you did the right thing, which was not bet a sure thing.

The realization that there WAS such an event as a sure thing had depressed Looney so much, his eyes were red. He had obviously been crying.

"Hear you had a big win," Vibes Eberhart said to Trotter, who shrugged.

Mickey Jax had collected his ten dollars for tipping a woman from Maine on the two horse, and even HE seemed upset with Trotter for having earned money so easily. Earned, hell. STOLE.

"So what's up?" Trotter asked the group as a whole.

He ordered a beer.

103

Nobody said a thing, even Evangeline, who had beer foam on her nose.

"Who does anybody like in the second?"

Vibes Eberhart sniffed.

Looney made noise through his teeth.

Mickey Jax squinted.

Trotter started to apologize for winning, but then thought better of it.

"Anybody want a beer?"

Everybody knew to the *penny* what Trotter had won. It was such an offensive amount, the purchase of a mere beer would only add insult to injury.

"Goddamn it, I TOLD you who I was going to bet. Every damn last one of you."

"So how's the weather," Vibes Eberhart said to Mickey Jax.

When Trotter's beer was placed on the counter, he realized he had made a frightful mistake.

"Still drinking beer?" Vibes Eberhart said. "Quaint."

Trotter realized he had put ALL of his money in his shoes and didn't have enough to buy his beer. He tried to borrow a buck from Vibes Eberhart. Failing, he took off his right loafer, removed a five, and told the bartender to give the boys (and Evangeline, who by now was almost one of the boys) a round on the house.

The boys said they passed.

He imagined that five thousand people watched his feet as he took his beer and retired to a bench to see what looked good on paper for the second.

Tony Cheeseburger squeezed in next to Trotter and asked, rather BEGGED, a hint of who Trotter liked.

"Here's five," Tony said. "Who you got?"

"That one," Trotter said at random. He had

pointed to a horse named Faith Healer.

Trotter took the five-dollar bill.

"I won't forget this," Tony said.

Tony Cheeseburger was Trotter's first groupie.

IT DAWNED ON TROTTER AS HE READ THE *Racing Form* that it was much harder to pick a winner starting from scratch than it was to pick a winner after hearing an optimistic prediction from a trainer on tape, a prediction that could be construed by certain members of the law-abiding community, like the racing stewards and district attorney, as cowardly, crooked, and just plain horseshit.

You wouldn't find *Trotter* taking the tape to the D.A. Nope. You don't find a couple hundred on the sidewalk and then start worrying if it's fake.

Trotter was loyal.

He would have done almost ANYTHING for the trainer.

So he didn't take the tape to the D.A. He did take it to the trainer, though.

THE STABLE AREA AT A TRACK IS NOT ONE OF THE GARden spots of America. The only resemblance between a garden spot and the stable is fertilizer. Nothing grows up from the fertilizer in a stable, though, except dreams.

To get to the stables, you have to show proper identification or you have to show a ten-spot, whichever comes first. Trotter hit the guy on the gate with a ten, and the guy was so overwhelmed by Trotter's credentials, he saluted.

There are rows of stalls full of horses, with the owners' colors and trademark, or brand, on the gate.

Jay Cronley

The horses have it good.

The people who work for the horses don't have it so good.

At most major tracks there are hot little dorms where people who walk, feed, and brush horses live, and it was in such a building Trotter poked his head.

Approximately 110 guys were shooting craps.

There were bunk beds around this room. It stunk to high heaven.

Craps is a game where dice are rolled. Trotter had played it more than once. But he had NEVER seen a crap game like this, where the game ended before the dice stopped rolling.

Some kid picked the dice up, mid-throw, and hit the door, almost knocking Trotter down. Trotter HAD participated in games where the dice had been sus-pect, like somebody thought they had jumping beans in them. But anybody questioning the veracity of the dice usually waited until the action had stopped.

"What was *that* all about?" Trotter asked a fellow who was chewing tobacco.

"Roscoe made himself five bucks, that's what."

Roscoe was the one who had scooped up the dice. They belonged to a man named Bottoms and the dice were coated with authentic sea shell, worth five, maybe six dollars.

"Oh," Trotter said.

The guy with the tobacco spit some on Trotter's shoe. It was no great loss. Still, Trotter would have just as soon been somewhere else.

"Where is Charity?" Trotter asked. "The horse that just won?"

The guy with the tobacco said, "It's funny when you talk about ROLLING dice. How the hell can something square roll?"

Trotter said he guessed it was like when somebody said let the good times roll. They were saying it hypothetically.

He was given directions to Charity's stall.

New dice were produced in the background.

Bets were made.

Somebody rolled twelve, craps.

That guy's life was threatened.

CHARITY HAD JUST REACHED HER STALL, AND WAS still being walked in front of it. She was still hot and bothered. The trainer was kissing the horse on her rump. He was so happy, he didn't hear Trotter say, "Hi, my name is Trotter."

He did, however, see the tape Trotter held.

Trotter was worried how he might phrase his request, but since the guy was not a real crook, and since this wasn't technically blackmail, he got through his short speech all right. Blackmail, Trotter assumed, was where you got something *real*. This wasn't blackmail.

This was air mail.

All he wanted was to shoot the breeze.

He explained the situation, which was: his acquaintance, Looney, had blundered into a little racing trivia that was accidentally recorded, here. Trotter held up the tape. The trainer, who was named Adams, hit his right fist in his left palm, the way Looney would do. Not as a threat. As a, "I knew something would go wrong," gesture.

"Don't worry," Trotter said. "Just give me a horse in the next race. You heard anything?"

Adams quickly considered his position. Here was a guy claiming, claiming nothing, here was a guy *with* a tape full of information that could get his trainer's license suspended. Why, Adams wondered, didn't the guy want money? The reason had to be the guy was mostly honest. He was also serious. All he wanted was a tip on a horse.

"That the tape?"

"Yeah," Trotter said.

Trotter had run across the street and had taken the tape from the Buick. Jake had seen Trotter. Trotter said the tape was his favorite Doris Day album. Jake bought the story.

Adams, the trainer, still wasn't sure what to make of this.

"Listen," Trotter said. "You already made me some money. I bet Charity, too. I feel bad about talking to you this way. Forget about the tape."

Trotter smashed it with his foot.

"It's the only one. If I was a blackmailer, I'd want money, right?"

Adams nodded, he guessed.

"I'm no crook," Trotter said.

"Neither am I," Adams said.

They shook hands warmly.

"I just needed some money," Adams said, "I THOUGHT we had it won. But you never know."

"I know," Trotter said. "I agree. No matter what you know, you never know."

"Exactly," Adams said. "That photo was unbelievable. The bastards had been holding Blurred Image back all year, same as us. She about ran out of her skin."

Trotter and Adams walked, arm in arm, toward the track.

"There's one in the next race that has a chance," Adams said. "I have a couple of bucks on him. The reason I think he has a chance is my jockey says the guy riding this next horse has a GRAND bet. The last grand that guy saw was the Grand Canyon. Must have borrowed it."

Trotter said it sounded good to him.

"That WAS the only tape?"

"Sure."

"Here," Adams said, handing Trotter some tickets. "It's a few extra box seats."

"Thanks," Trotter said.

"The one in the second race I like a little is named Faith Healer. You might put ten bucks on him. Who knows."

Trotter poked Adams in the ribs. Adams pinched Trotter's cheek.

Passers-by might have thought they were long-lost brothers.

THE HAMBURGER WAS TOUGH BECAUSE IT HAD A THIN slab of frozen ice in the middle, plus it was little, plus it was lousy.

Quinella Hogan tried to screw Trotter out of a quarter.

"And twenty-five cents makes two, and three is five," Quinella said.

"Yes it does," Trotter agreed. "Except the hamburger cost a dollar-fifty, so FIFTY should make two, not twenty-five."

"Oh," Quinella said. "Honest mistake."

The last honest mistake Quinella made was when she bent over to pick up what she hoped was a hastily thrown away two-dollar win ticket, leaving the hamburger stand in a state of chaos. Quinella never lets service stand in the way of earning a living.

Trotter's hamburger was placed on a piece of wax paper.

"Who you like?" Quinella asked.

Jay Cronley

"Faith Healer," Trotter said.

"Ironic," Quinella said. "I don't." What she probably meant was it was unusual when losers didn't agree. Trotter had read, in a brochure handed out at one of the Gamblers Limited meetings, where a study proved people usually bet their personalities. Guys who are a little cocky bet the favorites. Guys who are a little conservative bet the middle shots to place or show. Guys who don't win much tend to bet the underdogs. The same with football, and that kind of betting. Lufkin told Trotter once, in confidence, that he could tell which side of a bet a guy will take, nine times out of nine and a half. The shy guys take the dogs, the brash guys take the favorites.

"Sometimes," Lufkin whispered, "I play with them. Say the number is seven. I got this Cadillac salesman who thinks of himself as a real killer. Very aggressive. I make the number eight. He always takes the favorites. But I only play with jerks. You're no jerk."

Trotter remembered thanking Lufkin for not taking any more money than was necessary.

At Gamblers Limited, Trotter had figured last year, he lost $4,100 betting various sports.

"Why you like this Faith Healer?" Quinella asked Trotter as guys behind him in line acted like they were waiting for a table at Maxim's, and not a hamburger that felt like it was full of gravel.

"No real reason."

Quinella said she heard Trotter was hot. Trotter said he thought hot was where you won more than a race a year.

"You never know," Quinella said. "I've seen dumber guys than you hit two in a row."

Trotter looked at his hamburger. It could have passed for an Oreo.

"I just work here," Quinella apologized.

"You do?" somebody behind Trotter said.

Trotter told Quinella he would see her, and she said not if she saw him first, and he elbowed his way to the condiments shelf where a person could sometimes mash some mustard out of a container that was chained to a pole. The mustard container worked much the same as the sledgehammer game at the fair. You smash a lever, and if you're strong as an ox, you win one drop of mustard. Trotter worked himself into a panic getting the mustard.

To think a person could believe you were hot after hitting one lousy race. Had Trotter bet two dollars instead of fifty, he would be twenty-eight dollars up, and that isn't so hot.

Hotness, Trotter decided, is a matter of degree.

There are about thirty minutes between races, and the reason for this is quite simple. The more time between races, the more money people bet. They could run a race every ten minutes if they wanted to. They don't want to.

Cashing American Express travelers checks takes time.

Running across the street to one of a number of joints where personal checks are cashed takes time.

There is a blood bank a block and a half away. Giving blood takes time.

Trotter had time to dash to the stables to meet trainer Adams, to get a sandwich (made with 100 per cent Grade A sand), and to figure how much of his money to bet the second race.

One thing was for sure, Trotter was not going to behave the way he had in previous visits here.

There are so many rules of thumb about how to play when you're ahead, a guy has to bring gloves along, just to keep track. It's like having four or five eye-openers even though you've only got two eyes—it's legal to go with a couple or three rules of thumb at the track.

Forget:

Quit While You're Ahead.

That's for idiots.

It's for gamblers with pride, of which there are approximately four, and all are bingo players.

Play with the House's Money is not bad.

Actually, it's pretty good. When you go by that rule of thumb, chances are, your thumb's already broken, though. When you go with Play with the House's Money, you have to consider the over-all figure, not just what you lucked out today. To play with the house's money, including all of last year, Trotter would need in the neighborhood of four grand, one hundred, which is a very ritzy neighborhood—still on the other side of the tracks.

At least now, Trotter could SEE the tracks.

Before the first race, all he could see was the smoke from the engine.

Double up.

Triple up.

Quadruple up.

Take what you won the first race, divide by the humidity, and bet that on the horse carrying the most weight.

All systems, suggestions, and perversions look good on paper. So does Andrew Jackson's picture.

Trotter sat down and reconstructed days at the track where he got off to a fast start. It was not that difficult.

Once he hit a seventy-five-dollar Daily Double. He had placed this money in his right pocket, pledging to bet only ten dollars a race, from then on. He lost the next eight races to go home minus five.

He had done many things, like arranging money in the dark places of his body, so his winnings would be difficult to get at. Once, after a good start, and subsequent nickel and dime losses, Trotter was so frustrated, he lowered his trousers IN the two-dollar betting line to remove his last two bucks in time to bet the final race.

The only thing he had never done was let all of a win ride.

He checked the odds board. Faith Healer was the favorite at 3 – 1.

It takes a lot of guts to bet seven hundred dollars you just won.

Trotter wondered if he had any.

He had come with nothing and he had planned to go home with nothing, so if he lost, he would only be a half-hour late, was all.

The victory had taken a terrible toll on his social life.

Nobody was talking to him.

He did not feel at ease with the seven hundred dollars, really.

Maybe he WAS more comfortable with losing; he had lived with it so long. A person can UNDERSTAND losing. It stinks. Winning is hard to put your finger on.

Trotter guessed he felt guilty, after all, upsetting his friends.

He decided to let nature take its course.

He walked to the fifty-dollar window, where the seller congratulated Trotter on his unexpected but nevertheless impressive victory in the first race. Trotter heard none of it, for he was in the process of attempting to conjure up a major vibe.

He closed his eyes for a second.

"You all right?" the seller asked.

There were no words on a blackboard, but Trotter imagined a flash of his wife saying to a lawyer, "Go for his balls."

"Let it ride," Trotter said.

"Let what ride, on who?" the seller asked.

"Oh. Yeah."

Trotter removed his loafers and stacked the twenties on the counter.

"Welcome home," the seller said humorously.

"Wins on Faith Healer," Trotter said.

The seller said he would be damned. Most guys get lucky, they bet three dollars the next time.

The seller began ka-chunking the machine and fifty-dollar win tickets flew up.

Many of the tourists hanging in the background whispered, "Must be some oil baron."

"Dresses funny," somebody said.

"They're weird sometimes, the rich ones."

Trotter winked and tucked his knit shirt inside his jeans.

Ka-chunk, ka-chunk, ka-chunk. The machine ka-chunked out fourteen fifty-dollar tickets on Faith Healer.

As it was ka-chunking the last ones out, the sound reminded Trotter of an oil well.

He put the tickets in his front right pocket. The crowd behind the fifty-dollar window parted and Trotter marched through.

LOONEY CAUGHT TROTTER GOING DOWN THE STAIRS. He must have broken his blood oath with the others never to talk to Trotter again.

"Listen," he said. "I have an idea that will make us rich men."

His idea was to race across the street to the Buick

and get the tape and run to the stables and get Charity's trainer, Adams, and confront Adams with the damaging evidence. With what Adams won the first race, he wouldn't mind a bit paying Trotter and Looney something like ten grand for the tape, would he? Blackmail was not exactly Looney's cup of tea, but a person had to defend himself as life kept attacking.

Huh, Trotter.

When Trotter told Looney he had already destroyed the tape, Looney's mouth fell open. He grabbed at the sides of his face with his hands. He let out a horrible moan that scared hell out of a woman from Boston. She grabbed her heart.

Trotter told Looney that someday they would look back on this and laugh, and that although it didn't look like it now, Trotter had saved Looney from a life of crime and a lengthy jail sentence.

Looney would have hit Trotter, if he knew how.

Instead, he ripped the fifty dollars out of his pocket and stormed to the fifty-dollar window where he bet a 30–1 shot named June Bug, which was the name of Looney's cat.

IT WON, HANDS DOWN, EARS DOWN, FEET DOWN, AND tail down.

It was a horse-laugher.

Faith Healer stole the second race so easily the rest of the field couldn't have given a good description to the police artist.

It won going away. It won beyond a shadow of a doubt.

The nearest shadow to Faith Healer at the wire was the shadow of the grandstand.

It won beyond a REASONABLE doubt.

The damn horse won by ten lengths.

115

It broke clean, went on top, and won like it was running downhill. Faith Healer seemed mad the race had to end.

Some people couldn't believe it.

Trotter kind of believed it.

When the "Official" light was put on, he showed no emotion.

Simpson picked Trotter up by the elbows and kissed him on the forehead though.

Faith Healer paid seven dollars on a two-dollar win ticket.

That's nice.

Fourteen fifty-dollar win tickets paid two thousand four hundred and fifty dollars.

That's not nice.

That's real nice.

The cashier asked for, and received, Trotter's autograph. So did the I.R.S. You win so much money, you have to admit it, and sign forms.

This time, he was paid in one-hundreds, twenty-four of them, and one fifty-dollar bill.

"YOU'VE SHRUNK," VIBES EBERHART SAID.

Trotter did NOT say it was because he was walking on hundreds instead of twenties. Instead he said, "Yeah."

Tony Cheeseburger was on the verge of hysteria.

He had won seventy dollars on Trotter's tip, which had been made before Trotter even KNEW it was a tip, but it spends, you know?

Tony grasped Trotter by the shoulders and said, "I'm not going to forget this. I mean it."

Tony took a medallion from around his neck, leaving three, and he handed it to Trotter; Trotter was later to place it in Rudy's cigar box. "This means a lot to me, this medallion, even though it only cost four bucks—it's the thought, you know?" Tony said.

It was mock-gold and raised letters said, "Groovy."

When Trotter later placed the medallion in Rudy's cigar box after receiving a towel, Rudy was to say disgustedly, "I like money a hundred times better."

Quinella Hogan was so pleased with Trotter's tout on Faith Healer, she looked both ways and slipped Trotter a free hamburger. He took a bite, grabbed his jaw, and pitched the remainder of the sandwich at a garbage can. A guy loitering by the can grabbed the sandwich in mid-air and lost himself in the crowd before Trotter could so much as yell, "Watch your teeth!"

Trotter had eaten game birds like quail that had buckshot in them, but never a hamburger.

Trotter went downstairs, where none of the regulars usually wandered, and he collected his thoughts in a corner.

Now what? he wondered.

He had $2,450 in his shoes. His feet ached a little. It was probably gout with all that money down there.

Should I go home?

Should I bet two dollars on the next race?

Should I bet twenty dollars to see if I'm hot, or what?

There was a guy across the way, whispering to his buddy. The buddy nodded and pointed at Trotter. Those guys seemed to have just crawled from under a pile of garbage. Trotter tried to seem despondent, but he imagined he had a glow about him, a green aura with arrows pointing to his feet, arrows that looked like dollar signs.

It would be a shame to get robbed.

No sudden moves, Trotter decided. Those boys would be on him fast. Trotter lowered his head and walked over and asked the guys, "Got a buck so I can get a beer?"

"Are you crazy?" one asked.

"We was fixing to maybe come talk to you," the other guy said.

"Talk turkey," the first one said.

"Well, I'm tapped out," Trotter said shuffling his feet.

"You don't LOOK tapped," the first one said.

"You looked HAPPY," the other one said. "That was why we was going to talk to you."

Trotter said, "Well, sorry."

He lowered his head and shuffled off and the bums scouted around for another likely looking perfect stranger to borrow like seventy-five dollars from. Something somebody gives you without blood being shed, that's called borrowing.

There are two ways to keep from being robbed, Trotter decided.

The first way is to conceal the money in such a manner that when the robbers rip the clothes from your back, they won't find anything.

Trotter's old man had a secret pocket sewn in his shorts.

The other way to keep from being robbed is to stay away from robbers, like downstairs here, by the street entrance, where bums from across the way can crawl in from the bars.

He got into his pocket and removed the two box-seat tickets from trainer Adams, and sought immunity up there.

THESE WERE NOT YOUR RUN-OF-THE-MILL, CALL-SOME-rich-doctor box seats.

These were better than that. These were call-some-*politician* box seats. They were situated in the Jockey Club, which is a large room encased in glass, to keep the pests out. Waiters, carrying trays of food were everywhere, offering you snacks. A person snapped his fingers in the Jockey Club, a waiter would show up to take your wish, and another guy would show to mop your brow from the exertion.

These guys wore red.

Trotter showed his ticket to the man on the door, and the man on the door nodded gracefully and handed Trotter's stub to another man, who said, "This way."

Each box had six seats.

People were munching crisp things and pondering the *Racing Form* like they were at a library.

Four people were already in Trotter's box.

Trotter removed his right loafer and tipped the seating gentleman a buck. The guy nodded and walked away to wash the dollar.

"My name is Greenberg," a man in the box said, extending his hand to Trotter, "and I got more goddamn money than I know what to do with. My philosophy is, nobody knows you got money, what the hell is the use of having it?"

"Bernie is so silly," a blonde said.

Trotter said who he was, and sat down.

Rich people evidently didn't get too excited. This room was quiet.

Bernie Greenberg said to Trotter, "This is Miss Backstretch," of the blonde.

Trotter waited for the punch line and when none came, he took the blonde's fingers.

"I'm pleased," she said.

Trotter said nothing.

The blonde's breasts said it all. They were about to explode through a flimsy white blouse. The force of

119

this eruption would send buttons flying to the far corners of the Jockey Club.

Trotter cleared his throat eventually and said he didn't know they had a beauty contest at the track here, but he assumed it must be quite an honor to have won.

"He thinks you won a beauty contest," Bernie said.

"I could of, I think," the blonde said.

"And if you didn't, I would have bought it," Bernie said.

The blonde's name was appropriately enough Joy and she had been named Miss Backstretch at the annual meeting of chiropractors and leg-benders. Her blouse was open two buttons, just enough so that the waiters serviced this box with frequency and passion. There were guys popping in to perform such extra-curricular duties as cleaning underneath the table-cloth. A glimpse down Miss Backstretch's blouse was reward enough.

A diamond pendant hung precariously around her neck and over her breasts. If it fell, it would never be heard from again.

When Trotter said it was nice to meet her, he was looking at her breasts. He thought he heard an echo.

Jewels circled her wrists.

"What do you want in the third?" she asked Trotter.

Trotter was momentarily puzzled by the wording, but recovered in time to realize she was talking horses, maybe. He said he didn't know.

"Bernie lost his ass already," Miss Backstretch said.

It was like a night club. There was a table. To Trotter's left was the finish line. The Jockey Club was a level above the grandstand so members of the peanut gallery wouldn't nauseate everybody by climbing up and pressing their faces on the glass. Beneath the table, a shoeless foot was rubbed against Trotter's shin. Maybe a waiter checking for dead flies, Trotter guess-hoped. He doubted it.

Bernie was in envelopes. His company made them for greeting cards of all sizes, including a joke envelope that was three feet by five feet, which cost $19.95.

"How many you want?" Bernie asked Trotter, whose loafer was being removed by a very talented foot. When the shoe was free, two feet began massaging Trotter's ankle and calf.

"Six," Trotter said.

"You got it." Bernie Greenberg wrote Trotter an order for a half-dozen three-foot by five-foot envelopes. Trotter signed the receipt, and was told to allow four to six weeks for delivery.

His right leg was in heaven.

Miss Backstretch was still wearing her neutral smile. Maybe it was the only one in her repertoire.

Nobody except midgets had ever touched Trotter's leg at the track before.

A slight grin had crept across his face. It was all he could do to refrain from crawling under the table to see exactly what was up.

Bernie was about fifty-five.

Miss Backstretch couldn't have been more than twenty-one. Her breasts were much younger. Parts of them, the sides especially, looked about two years old. They had obviously been given a helping hand or needle somewhere along the way.

Trotter raised a hand for a drink.

Bernie said he'd just bought a townhouse on the east side, one with an elevator, that cost so much, it took them six hours to add up all the sales tax. He had a place on the west side he sold for a 700 per cent profit.

"Was a dice game in front of it all the time," Miss Backstretch said of the old place. "It just stayed there, guys speaking funny languages. Very scary. I'm glad Bernie moved."

Miss Backstretch said she put five dollars in the crap game pot as a tip every time she came or went, so those guys wouldn't knife her. Bernie said so THAT'S why the game never moved!

As she talked, her feet continued to slip up and down Trotter's calf.

"Guess how many bedrooms I got?" Bernie asked Trotter.

Trotter didn't know.

"I don't KNOW how many I got, THAT'S how many!"

"That's a lot," Trotter said.

"We've found six," Miss Backstretch said without so much as a blush.

The other people at the end of this table, to Trotter's right, were in their fifties, and they were discussing the upcoming race, but with great calm and reserve. The man had been so discomforted at losing the last race, he said he was going to get even by wagering a thousand this time.

Trotter assumed he meant dollars. Maybe he meant a thousand million. Who the hell knew in this room.

There is a tendency to pay more attention to a person's choice of horses if he's betting a grand. But since a grand to that guy was like a ten to somebody normal, Trotter resisted the urge to eavesdrop on this man's choice, and he instead returned his eyes to Miss Backstretch's buttons. He discreetly scooted about an inch lower in his chair. The feet squeezed his knee.

The waiter arrived for Trotter's wish.

"Tom Collins."

"He's off today," the waiter said. "That's a little joke, sir." He wrote Trotter's request on a pad with a gold pen.

Miss Backstretch excused herself to use the rest room. She had long legs. They went all the way from her rear to the floor.

The blouse held.

Approximately thirty-two waiters said, almost together, "My God."

Somebody at the table behind Trotter tapped him on the back. It was a woman, a very thin, well-dressed woman, who said, "Have you a pen I could borrow?"

Her hand rested on Trotter's shoulder.

Something like a cube of ice was on her ring finger.

She smelled like peaches.

Another perfectly dressed woman was across the table from this one.

Trotter handed her a pen and asked, "Can I get you something to drink?"

"I don't know why not, I take the pill," she said.

Trotter blinked.

He ordered some rum for her. She squeezed his shoulder and turned around, back to the *Racing Form*.

Bernie winked at Trotter. "Mrs. Davis. Real classy, you know?" He leaned across the table toward Trotter. "Her husband owns a few hundred horses. Don't worry, he's usually out of town."

Trotter had never been at the races when winning was secondary to things like lust.

He snacked on lobster, sipped good whiskey, relieved himself from the pressure of picking a winner in the *Form* by looking at a variety of breasts, and told a waiter it was all right there was a smudge on the ash tray.

Bernie Greenberg had absorbed so much information from the *Form* concerning the third race, his eyes started to bug out.

When he got up to bet, Miss Backstretch scooted closer to the table and rested her leg on Trotter's knee.

The woman who looked like she just stepped off the cover of *The Best of Vogue* had turned to watch the horses come on the track for the third race. She placed her right hand on the seat of Trotter's chair, and moved her fingers so they touched his leg.

Only when he saw the horses parade past the Jockey Club, he saw them GOOD because the glass was spotless, did he remember what he was here for.

THE PROBLEM WITH WINNING, IN ADDITION TO THE comfortable style of life it encourages, which really isn't a problem, it's more of an addiction, is that after a person has lucked out a couple, he begins to think of himself as some sort of wise guy, or even genius.

It's only natural.

You forget you won because you kind of broke the law twice—the tape and the blackmail, or at least the gray-mail—so all you remember is you have a pocketful of cash, and the next thing you know is you're sitting there studying the *Racing Form*, like YOU got the first two winners, which you didn't.

Unfortunately, Trotter fell into this trap.

He forgot what had buttered his bread.

Surrounded by the style and grace of the Jockey

Club, where people had so much dough it didn't make a damn if they had inside information because it didn't make a damn if they lost, Trotter began thinking he was good at picking horses. He had three or four drinks and made sophisticated jokes, like the one to the beautiful thin woman who had her fingers under his leg.

When she said, "I find it difficult to bet on odd-numbered horses," Trotter said, "Call off your dogmas."

Trotter had a pretty good whiskey glow when he rose to bet his selection for the third race, which ironically enough was a horse named Lord Byron. That fit the over-all mood of this room; it was poetic.

Plus, Trotter concluded silently, Lord Byron could run. He was the 2–1 favorite, but when you have hundreds or more to bet, small pay-offs are terribly worthwhile.

And Trotter was hot.

He couldn't lose.

He could bet a three-legged horse and it would figure a way to win.

He had come with fifty bucks and he was sitting on, rather standing on, almost two grand and a half.

Things happen for a reason. The reason Trotter was ahead was because it was in the cards for him to become MORE ahead. The deck, clearly, was stacked.

Plus, Lord Byron could run.

The next best thing to having God on your side was having a good horse on your side.

You had both, well, it's time for more salmon eggs.

Trotter was looking at five thousand dollars.

He felt giddy as he got up and walked through the Jockey Club. He felt confident. He was going to bet the whole amount on Lord Byron. He excused himself to Bernie, to Miss Backstretch, and to the ladies with tweed blood.

Here's how confident Trotter was:

He ordered a round of drinks for both tables, to be paid for with winnings from this race.

Before, he would have rat-holed enough for a beer.

IT IS AMAZING HOW QUICKLY A PERSON CAN SOBER UP, from drunkenness; or sober down, from a mild high.

Trotter was in complete control of his faculties by the time the handcuffs were clicked shut.

They hurt.

"What's going on here?" he said. That was what most criminals said when the cuffs were put on, but he couldn't do any better on such short notice.

"Is this a joke?"

That's the *next* thing criminals say. Trotter had put enough cuffs on guys during his brief stay as guardian of the law to know how the criminal mind works.

The third thing they usually say is, "That hurts," and then sometimes they say, "What do I get if I turn my best friends in?"

"That hurts," Trotter said, and the two guys who had cuffed him smiled to each other, well, there's another criminal element off the streets. Even though Trotter didn't volunteer to turn in his accomplices, the two guys figured they had him dead to rights.

"Let me go bet Lord Byron," Trotter said, wiggling his shoulders so they wouldn't break.

The two cops had to admire a guy like that, going down swinging.

"You got a lot of moxie," one cop said, showing

Trotter identification. His name was Rogers. "But you're still under arrest."

"Why?" Trotter asked. "Tell me why I'm under arrest. Why?"

Trotter's rights were read, in front of several hundred people, one of whom was Vibes Eberhart. None of the rights Trotter was read was the right to bet.

"Let's go, Morgan," the cop named Rogers said to Trotter.

"I'm not Morgan."

"He's not Morgan," the cop named Rogers said to the other one. "What do you think?"

The other cop looked at a piece of paper and then at Trotter. He nodded, "I say he is."

"Me too," Rogers said. "You lose, 2−1."

"I'm not Morgan, God damn it."

"Swearing in public is against the law," Rogers said.

"So is false arrest," Trotter said.

"You're not under arrest," Rogers said. "You're only handcuffed for questioning."

There were only ten minutes remaining before post time for the third race. Trotter yelled at Vibes Eberhart, who was taking the action in without emotion.

"Vibes, tell them who I am," Trotter begged.

Vibes Eberhart turned around and walked off.

"I'll kill you for that," Trotter screamed, which did his chances for on-the-spot acquittal no good, so the cops led Trotter past the betting windows to a little room where two other cops were reading a *Racing Form*.

"We got Morgan here," Rogers said.

"That's interesting," one cop said. "Who do you

127

like in the third?" The issue was discussed as precious minutes vanished in mid-air.

"Crime doesn't pay," Rogers said to Trotter. Since Trotter had come to the track with no identification, since he had slightly more than $2,400 in his shoes, he was restricted as to his next move. One thing was for sure, it had to count. He imagined Lord Byron lapping the field.

Trotter put one and one together and it came out two years, minus time out for good behavior.

One minute he had been rubbing hobnobs with the hopelessly rich in the Jockey Club, and the next he was in cuffs. He had been walking to the fifty-dollar window to make a bet when these two comedians had accosted him, and without warning, so here he was, being called Morgan. The horses were probably taking their last jogs before lining up to enter the gate. The last Trotter had seen, as these clowns shoved him toward this room, Lord Byron was three to two. This fiasco was costing him five thousand dollars. It was a case of mistaken identity. The money in his shoes would be very hard to explain. It couldn't be done in three minutes, which was about how much was left until post time.

"Listen, I'm not Morgan," Trotter said as a last resort.

All four cops were reading the *Form*. "Be quiet," one of them said.

So be it.

Trotter had no choice except to spring into action, which he did without any problem, since his feet weren't shackled. He leaped to his feet and ran for the door and blasted it open with his right shoulder. This put him back in business. He ran down the hallway and banged open another door and came out on the second level of the track, next to Quinella Hogan's beer stand.

Footsteps and words followed him.

"Blast him," one cop said.

Rogers said, "Put your gun away, you can't shoot no pickpocket!"

So that's who they thought he was.

Hell with them.

"What's your hands doing handcuffed?" Quinella Hogan yelled at Trotter. The sudden appearance of a handcuffed man set off a medley of shrieks and screams like, "My God, there's a killer loose!"

Trotter ran for the betting window. It's very hard to run with your hands cuffed because you tend to lean forward. Trotter bounced off a few people, like he was running through a pinball game.

"Maybe they're shooting a commercial," somebody said. "Like O. J. Simpson at the airport."

Rogers and the other three cops were pushing after Trotter, yelling, "Stop that man." Thank God people are rotten, Trotter thought, and wouldn't throw a cup of ice at a baby snatcher.

The cops were tangled in the crowd. The fifty-dollar window was just around the corner. He was going to make it, get his bet down. THEN explain to those meatballs what a mistake they had almost made.

Trotter ran up a dozen steps, three at a time. There was nobody at the window! There was still time!

"Stop that man," the cop named Rogers shouted again.

Trotter saw somebody, some THING coming at him from off to the right. It was a blur. It reminded him of his football days in high school when guys tried to break your knees with a block. It was a Good Samaritan who had given up his body in order to stop an escaping criminal.

The psychopath had thrown his body at Trotter's legs.

Trotter jumped, straight up.

This maneuver had worked many times in high school. It was too bad he didn't have the same legs, though, fifteen years later here.

The Samaritan's shoulders clipped Trotter's feet.

The hero went on under Trotter and crashed into a wall.

Trotter landed on his right side and began rolling toward the fifty-dollar window, like a dog. He reminded himself of one of those *corn* dogs they roll in batter before dipping in grease.

He rolled and rolled and rolled and bumped against the base of the fifty-dollar window.

He struggled to his knees and looked up wide-eyed at the ticket seller.

A loud bell rang and somebody said over a loudspeaker so the sellers could act accordingly, "The third race is now closed."

This means that the only thing you could get a bet on was how old the hamburgers were.

"And, they're off," the race announcer said. "It's Lord Byron breaking on top, followed by Miss Match."

"You can't win them all," Looney said, getting to his feet.

He was the one who had tackled Trotter.

Before Trotter could ask why, even before Trotter could place his cuffed hands around Looney's neck and squeeze, Trotter was confiscated by the long, but nervous—since jobs were on the line when a criminal escaped—arm of the law.

It all came out in the wash.

CASES OF MISTAKEN IDENTITY ARE THOROUGHLY checked out because false arrest has become the flip side of malpractice. There are guys, and women, who pretend to shoplift things so they can be falsely arrested and start suing.

Trotter hoped the mess could be settled without the assistance of his good friends in the Jockey Club. The waiters in red might faint, having an alleged criminal in their presence.

There had been a guy named Morgan picking pockets and snatching purses and his description sort of matched Trotter's.

Trotter was returned to the room and his feet were cuffed to the table and explanations and alibis were offered. Trotter's erratic behavior, innocent people don't usually run for it, was caused by the hot streak he was enjoying. If this were true, the cops could understand that.

Trotter told them where they could go.

They did.

The cops interviewed the cashier at the fifty-dollar window and learned that Trotter had indeed won two big ones equalling the cash in his shoes.

Trotter's identity was verified.

"Don't call home," he had requested.

The cops didn't. One of them had a nervous wife, too. They called the cab company. Trotter was Trotter.

Looney, who had flipped out, more or less, had been interviewed, and his testimony had been dismissed as that of a sore loser. He had lost his fifty dollars when he bet the long shot with the same name of his cat. He had been hitting the whiskey with both hands. He blamed Trotter for his various misfortunes.

"Should have blamed his cat," Trotter told the cops, who smiled.

Looney had testified that Trotter was an escapee from a mental institution where he had been committed for cannibalism. The cops determined that Looney was drunk, so they led him to the front gate and deposited him on the sidewalk. The cop named Rogers said Looney was last seen walking irrationally in the direction of the blood bank.

After matters were resolved, and it was proved conclusively that Trotter was not a pickpocket named Morgan, and it was proved that Trotter WAS in the throes of a hot streak, you would have thought Trotter would have harbored some ill-feeling toward these idiotic cops. But nothing was more removed from the truth.

When Trotter was given a clean bill of conscience, he invited the four track cops to his private box in the Jockey Club, where he ordered and PAID for, a round of fancy mixed drinks. More importantly, as a GENUINE display of his friendship, Trotter introduced the cops to Miss Backstretch, who said, "I'm pleased."

Miss Backstretch had a winner the last race and her chest was filled with pride, and the blouse seemed to be hanging over her breasts by a single thread.

"What was THAT all about?" Bernie Greenberg asked Trotter, of the cops.

"Friends," Trotter said.

It was true. The same could be said of Looney, poor fellow. Trotter would have to send a runner to the blood bank to head Looney off with a twenty, anonymously, of course.

Guys who give blood to bet at the track have pride.

Lord Byron was beaten like a drum.

Trotter had seen the replay in the room where he had been detained while the cops checked things.

Lord Byron broke fast, as the track announcer had said, and all was well around the first turn. But along the back way, the jockey had fallen off during a shocking episode of bumping. The jockey rolled along the ground like a tumbleweed. Lord Byron jogged on around the track, much to the displeasure of the thousands who had bet their grocery money on his pretty nose.

The horse that had bumped Lord Byron was disqualified.

Lord Byron wasn't in the money because it's a rule, you have to have a jockey.

Fortunately, everybody concerned emerged uninjured, ESPECIALLY Trotter.

You talk about the fear of God, though.

Had Trotter not been mistaken for a pickpocket, had Looney not sideswiped him, Trotter would be back broke. He wouldn't be sitting here in the Jockey Club, toasting God, motherhood, and breasts. He would be busted.

Tapped out.

There is a fine line that separates winning and losing, isn't there?

The fact that Trotter STILL couldn't pick a horse using the *Racing Form* and his own wits was overshadowed by the more memorable fact that he should have lost, but didn't.

Not losing can be more exciting than winning. And the way Trotter had avoided losing was further evidence that he was on a hot streak, maybe.

The line that separates winning and losing can be as subtle as the line of your jawbone, which might remind a cop of a pickpocket.

"And here's to the horse you rode in on," Trotter toasted.

TROTTER WAS PAGED AGAIN AND HE DECIDED TO TAKE it on the white phone in the Jockey Club. The phone was located behind the cash register, which was about to come apart at the seams.

Drinks were $3.50 a head in here.

Beers were $1.00 a head and $1.00 for the body.

There were not many things in the Jockey Club that reminded Trotter of the outside, except the desire to break even. The times he had glanced in here, he had assumed that the rich get richer; that losers lost; that winners won.

That is not quite the case.

After the third race, nobody around Trotter was ahead, with the exception of Miss Backstretch. She had taken her winnings from the last race and had coyly stuffed it down her blouse with as much modesty as possible.

The blouse was taxed to the limit. The threads were stretched like ropes used for tug-of-war.

Any minute now, there would be something to tell your grandchildren.

Bernie Greenberg was in the pot to the tune of about six hundred bucks. He had dedicated his heart and soul toward getting even. It was the *principle* of the thing.

At the track, there are several spin-offs of the old saw, It takes money to make money.

Outside, where guys get sunburned veins, they've given so much blood at the blood bank and at the windows, they think:

It takes money to break even.

Nobody really expects to win out there. The more money you have, the more chances you have to break even. Out there, hope springs eternal in the human breast pocket; you got a ten-spot in there, you can play the 30–1 shot and get even.

Up here in the fancy-pants section where ladies wear mink even though it's 74 degrees, the prevailing opinion concerning the over-all philosophy of money's role in society is:

Another round.

Whereas the track is considered an "opportunity" by those downstairs, a way to once in a while make the rent money, up here, it's more "entertainment." These people didn't make their fortunes at the track, they made them in the business world.

Now if a Bernie Greenberg plops six hundred dollars on some dog, and it wins, he's not going to give it back. He'll keep it and buy some house plants.

But if he loses a goodly sum, which happens more often than not, well, here's where racing can have an adverse effect on the average guy struggling along out there, driving a cab, selling Bibles, whatever. If a Bernie Greenberg gets in big trouble and loses a small fortune, he gets it back by jacking up the prices of his envelopes.

That's sad, but that's also life.

The next time you're at the track and you glance into a club where the big-hitters are smoking Fidel Castro autographs, just remember, the price of envelopes or bananas or shoes may depend on whether or not some guys pick a winner.

Bernie Greenberg planned to bet a grand the fourth race. He had already taken into consideration the possibility he might lose that, and in doubling up to catch up, many more grands this day. He began adding a half-cent to the price of his birthday envelope inventory. That's known as insurance.

Miss Backstretch was playing Trotter's calf like a piano, with her toes.

There was a guy down the way who owned four cafeterias. He was taking a bath. The roast beef would be up a nickel a whack, come Monday. Inflation. Yeah, sure. Inflation of the head. The guy had some slide-rule gadget and thought he could use it to pick winners.

The only thing Trotter had difficulty adjusting to was the lack of emotion in the Jockey Club, except when Miss Backstretch sighed or made her way to the powder room. When a horse crossed the finish line, it was like you were watching a play.

The other fringe benefits more than made up for the stuffy attitude, though.

Trotter smiled at Miss Backstretch.

She squeezed his leg.

Bernie Greenberg did some more figuring and said to Miss Backstretch, "Take a letter."

"B," she said.

Trotter had never been unfaithful to his wife of seven years, but then, all good things must come to an end.

"Do I win?" Miss Backstretch asked. "I guessed B."

Bernie Greenberg explained that in addition to her duties as back-fixer for a chiropractor, Miss Backstretch did part-time secretarial work for the envelope king.

"I file things," she said, winking at Bernie. "Like my nails."

TROTTER GOT UP TO ANSWER THE PAGE, WHICH WAS getting on his nerves. It was probably one of the guys playing an impractical joke.

The guys, that was funny. Marty. Eberhart. Sid Booten and Evangeline. Tony. Quinella. Mickey Jax. Solly Friedman. Shiela the Salvation Navy lady. Looney. It was like Trotter hadn't seen them in YEARS.

"Come back," Miss Backstretch said.

"Okay," Trotter said.

The single button standing between Miss Backstretch and immortality vibrated with strain. She had a sip of beer. The floodgates held one more time. All it would take was one mosquito bite in the right place, and it would be all over.

A waiter in red wiped the phone clean with a cloth before handing it to Trotter.

"Yeah," Trotter said.

"I knew it, you bastard," was the reply from the other end of the phone.

Trotter closed his eyes and quickly tried to think of a way out of the trap he had so ignorantly blundered into. All he could think of to say was, "Hi, Pam."

"I knew it, you bastard," was the reply once again.

"Is this a recording?" Trotter asked humorously.

One did not have a fight with one's mate in the Jockey Club. It wasn't cricket.

"I'm through," Pam said.

"Now, Pam."

"Don't Pam me, you bum."

137

"I am no bum."

Trotter started to put a waiter on the phone to testify as to his improved status.

"You are a lying, rotten, inconsiderate bum."

Trotter didn't have to take this.

"And I'm leaving," Pam said.

Well, maybe he should take a LITTLE of it.

"And I'm going to file for divorce and take every penny you've got or ever will have. I'm going to skin you alive."

Trotter decided not to hang up just yet.

He smiled and nodded into the phone so the waiters might think he was talking to his broker or something.

Pam continued:

"You're going to pay for what you've put me through, and I want you to know it. You're at your precious track. Well, while you're there, I want you to think every second about what it's going to be like living at the Y with all the perverts. We've been married a long time so I can get alimony. I can get it all. I will."

"Um, pork bellies don't sound too good," Trotter said as waiters whizzed by, nodding understandably.

One waiter said, "Good move. Soybeans are the play."

Trotter nodded.

"You're drunk," Pam said.

Divorce was not one of Trotter's favorite subjects because a guy named Shinn had got that last week. Shinn's wife took everything but his appendix. He is currently sleeping in his cab, which gets a little old, particularly when punks try to turn it over at three in the morning.

The way the divorce laws are these days, a guy is lucky to get out with his bowling balls. Shinn told

Trotter the way it works when you go to trial contest-
ing various things is the judge decides on the alimony, child support, and property settlement. Shinn
says if you've been married a long time and have kids
(or dogs), and if the alleged wife doesn't work, what
happens then is the judge gives the wife the house,
car, kids, and everything but the bowling balls. Shinn
says it's kind of hard using a bowling ball for a pillow.
When Shinn asked the judge if it was all right to take
a pillow, the judge laughed, rapped his gavel, and
said, "No."

Shinn said another interesting aspect of the divorce law is a woman can sue you for being ugly, and
call it something else, like incompatibility. What's
grim is when you fight it and your wife gets up and
testifies what a rat you are. Shinn said what's best is
to give up, fake a heart attack, and then maybe your
ex will leave a pillow. You fight it, you're chopped
liver.

Trotter thought of Shinn sleeping in his cab and
said to his wife, "I'm not drunk at all."

"I KNEW you were at the track," Pam said. "I
KNEW you were lying. I KNEW you were gambling.
You're sick."

Even though Pam didn't want to talk about it, she
briefly mentioned some of the highlights of Trotter's
gambling career, like the time he bet on a high school
basketball game, which was similar to child molesta-
tion, and the time he kicked the television in, and the
times, the thousands of times, he stayed up all night
on the roof of the apartment trying to pick up football
and basketball games played in faraway places. Pam
also mentioned the times Trotter had made a bet and
couldn't wait for the score, and called the gym and
had a guy leave the phone open, there on the press
table, all the last half. This call cost sixty-nine dollars,

plus Trotter lost the fifty-five dollar bet. Had he won, he would still have lost money. Pam remembered all the low points, like taking a transistor radio to the ballet.

"It's amazing," she said, "I stayed around this long."

Trotter said nothing.

"I told you if you gambled one more time, I was leaving."

"But I'm not gambling," Trotter said weakly.

"What are you doing then, picking pockets?"

"I'm winning."

Trotter waited for the phone to be slammed off. When it hadn't happened in fifteen seconds, he said, "Really."

"Really what?"

"Really I'm winning."

He explained what had happened, how he had steamrolled a pittance into fifty times that. He told his wife that he was currently sitting in a box in the Jockey Club, and he was surrounded by some of the business leaders who make this great country tick.

"Maybe one of them can give you a job so you won't have to drive that stinking cab anymore," Pam said.

"Yeah, right. Probably. For sure."

Trotter explained that he was on a roll and couldn't lose. What was happening today would erase the bad memories forever. Stick with him, he pleaded, just once more.

"Where's the money?" Pam asked.

"In my shoes."

"Are you lying? Again?"

"No."

Trotter threw himself at his wife's mercy. He *realized* what was at stake. He WAS, as hard as it was to believe, winning. After he explained in detail about

Lord Byron, Pam relaxed slightly and asked if Trotter had eaten anything.

"Only caviar."

"We *could* use the money," Pam said.

Trotter agreed.

"I'm leaving," she said.

"No!"

"To come join you."

"Oh," Trotter said. He about dropped the phone. "To come join me?"

"Yes. Don't make another bet until I get there."

"To come join me?" Trotter gave her his box number.

"Don't get drunk and blow it," Pam said. "I'm leaving now. I'll be there in a half-hour."

Trotter didn't know what to say.

"We could use some more money," Pam said. "If you're really winning."

"I'm streaking," Trotter said.

"You know what worries me?" Pam asked.

Trotter didn't know anything.

"Mr. Love at the gamblers' place said it was impossible to win at the track. Said in the end, you always lose."

"There are no robbers wearing sacks on their heads here, Pam."

"Be careful, honey," Pam said. "What should I wear?"

Trotter said something that flowed.

They hung up.

Within seconds, Trotter was outraged. All these years, he thought it was GAMBLING his wife despised. But what she hated was LOSING!

Trotter was not sure what this startling turn of events, this shocking change of heart on his wife's part, meant, exactly.

141

Seats on the bandwagon did not come cheap.

Trotter ordered a triple rum something that came out smelling like cologne.

He went to the bathroom in the Jockey Club.

The wallpaper was a collage of *Wall Street Journals*.

LUFKIN'S ARRIVAL WAS A THING OF BEAUTY.

It was something Busby Berkeley would have envied.

Johnny Casino came down the steps like a mine sweeper, clearing a path for Lufkin. Two apes brought up the rear. Lufkin tipped his fedora to various ladies and plopped into his box seat.

A fedora is a hat.

Johnny Casino collects for Lufkin when all other measures have failed. He's got a little laugh that sounds like chalk scraping across a blackboard. Johnny Casino visited Trotter once and threatened to cut Trotter's ears off because he was late with some money. A horrible mistake had been made. Trotter had settled up on time; his sheet had been confused with another guy's who lived in the same apartment. Trotter showed Johnny Casino how the error had occurred and escorted the weasel to the proper apartment, where a man named Brubaker had locked himself in the bathroom. Trotter went back home as Johnny Casino prepared to hurl a color television through Brubaker's bathroom door.

Johnny Casino used to work Vegas until he made a slight mistake. He worked for a gambling joint, providing refreshment for the big-hitters on markers. When they got way behind, he would refresh their memories.

Some orthodontist from Dallas ran up a whale of

a tab so Johnny Casino made his usual pep talk, which was, "Hey, punk, it's my idea you should make some of these markers good or else I might have to feed you to the desert, you understand?"

Frank Sinatra said, "What?"

The orthodontist from Dallas DID look a little like Sinatra, in all that smoke in the gambling room.

It was still a *bad* mistake.

Johnny Casino was asked to please leave Las Vegas, which he did, fast, not twenty minutes after he had mistaken Frank Sinatra for a deadbeat orthodontist.

Lufkin hired Johnny Casino as vice president in charge of keeping track.

Lufkin and his entourage sat in a box behind Trotter.

When Johnny Casino saw Trotter, he checked a book and sent a note down:

You owe some money from last week.

Trotter returned what he had lost on football, along with a five-dollar tip for Johnny with the message:

Get your shoes vacuumed.

Johnny wore shoes made of material, like suede, to match his suit color. The shoes he was wearing today were purple.

Johnny reddened and whispered something to Lufkin, probably requesting permission to throw Trotter through the plate glass, and Lufkin shook his head.

"Where's your friend Looney?" Lufkin asked.

"He's late with some money," Johnny said. "Bad late." He flipped through some pages in his book. "Sickeningly late."

Trotter said he didn't know.

"Hundreds late."

Various envelopes were collected by a waiter from other members of the Jockey Club, and they were placed neatly in front of Lufkin. Bernie Greenberg wrote Lufkin a check for eleven hundred dollars.

"Bernie," Lufkin said, "I swear to God, I hate this. It makes my stomach hurt. A guy like you, though, is on the verge at all times. Next week, it's me giving you this back, I got a feeling in my bones."

"You never know," Bernie said.

"I know," Lufkin said. "You got a good glow to your face, Bernie. Not high blood pressure or anything like that. A healthy glow. I'll tell you what, though, that Ivy League football, you just got to stay with it, outlast it. Believe me, those guys getting three scores in the last five minutes was a real crime. Christ, the way they score, you need an adding machine. This is a new kind of envelope, Bernie?"

Lufkin removed the check.

"Fairly," Bernie said.

Lufkin ordered a couple thousand.

"They just went up a nickel a dozen," Bernie said.

"Hey, whatever's fair."

Lufkin did some bookkeeping and prepared to leave. He asked Trotter to walk him to the door. "Races make me nervous," Lufkin said. "You can't win. Listen, I tell you this like an uncle. You're a little up, take off. You can't beat those things."

He nodded toward the track.

"We thought we'd find you at the dump across the street," Johnny Casino said. "That dump where pigs wallow. Not up here."

"You thought wrong," Trotter said. "Nice shoes. Where the hell you get them, a carpet sale?"

"I hope some day you're two seconds late with the money," Johnny said.

"You remember the old saying," Trotter said, smiling. Money seemed to give him courage.

"What?"

"Dead men can't pay up."

"Crippled men can," Johnny said.

"Your friend Looney is in a little trouble," Lufkin said. "Well, more than a little. He bet the Giants today."

Trotter said, "So?"

"He bet them pretty hard."

"They lost one seventy-five to ten," Johnny said.

"Forty-five to ten," Lufkin corrected him. "Same difference, though. Your pal Looney, he went for a nickel."

Trotter couldn't believe it. A nickel is five hundred dollars. Looney had said he only bet fifty dollars.

"So," Lufkin said, "he's down eight something."

Johnny said, "Which is a lot for a bum."

Lufkin asked that if Trotter saw Looney, please pass along the message:

Pay up.

"Here's a P.S.," Johnny said. "Or else."

Trotter doubted he would see Looney.

"Whatever," Lufkin said. "Listen, do me a favor. Go on home. You look like you might be up a little. Nobody wins here."

"Take it and bet football with you, right?"

"There's TWO teams. There's like TWELVE horses. Figure it yourself. Here, you're outnumbered. Here, a guy gets hot, there's some more races, he can't quit, right? Listen to me. I would a lot rather trust my money with a fullback that's got a master's degree in business than a dumb goddamn horse that don't even understand English. How much you up?"

"Some," Trotter said.

"Go home," Lufkin said. "I know a guy that came to the track with twenty lousy bucks, hit six in a row, and was up five grand. Bets the next one and the dumb horse loses by a fraction so the guy, named

145

Griffin, remember him, Johnny? the guy goes off the deep end, right in the Hudson. There's enough horse players down there, hell, the river's three feet higher this time of year."

Trotter thanked Lufkin for the advice and went to use the phone. It was taken. He left the Jockey Club and ran across the street to Marty's to use the pay phone there.

Sid Booten and Evangeline were having a beer.

"We lost the hell out of things," Sid said.

"The sons of bitches killed us," Evangeline said. She was *officially* one of the boys. She was also a little drunk. "There's jockeys at this track couldn't stay on a merry-go-round, huh, Sid."

"Damn right, Evangeline."

"Let's have another beer, Sid."

"Okay, Evangeline."

"I don't know much about horses but it seems to me you get ON a horse, you would have the common decency to STAY on. What I want to know Sid is how come when the jockey falls off, they still take your money? That's what I want to know."

"It's a rule," Sid Booten said.

"It's a stupid rule. What time is it, Sid?"

It was about a quarter of three.

"I may go by the bank, Sid," Evangeline said. "I may go by the bank and draw some savings out and come back here and get back what we lost. What do you think about that, Sid? How much we lose?"

"Counting the beer?"

"All of it."

"Eighty, ninety. Not much."

"I'm pretty mad, Sid, let me tell you that."

After languishing in the Jockey Club, Trotter felt like a medic that followed behind the front lines, taking pulses and counting bodies. The smoke stung his eyes. One guy was smoking in his sleep.

"You seen Looney?" Trotter asked.

"Is this on or off the record?" Sid Booten asked.

"Looney said you were a real jerk," Evangeline said.

"Then you HAVE seen him."

"Looney said you turned on your friends."

"He went to give blood," Sid Booten said.

"Why don't we go do that, Sid?" Evangeline said. "It would save us a trip to the bank. I'm pretty mad, the way that jockey fell off."

Sid Booten said that Lufkin was in a few minutes ago looking for Looney. They told Lufkin that Looney had joined the Salvation Army and was shipped to Kansas to open a mission. Lufkin left a phone number Looney was supposed to call. Lufkin carved the number on one of the tables in Marty's.

Marty was not his old self.

He was having a hard time realizing that one of his whammies had come in as good as second.

There was a guy on the pay phone at the end of the bar, saying, "This is what I get for calling you, right? I get this. I get a kick in the teeth. I don't care what you say, Ruth, those are NOT pool balls you hear. I told you, I'm at the hospital. A guy at work falls off a beam, right? So I come here with him, that's why I'm late. He about dies, and this is what I get. I'll tell the poor guy when he wakes up, IF he wakes up, you don't believe he fell off the beam. I'm at the Emergency Room, Ruth. The guy is in there, dying, losing blood. Here's the number if you don't believe me. It's 747-2202. That's right. Well, the hell with you, Ruth. Go ahead and leave. See if the judge says taking a guy who falls off a beam to the hospital is grounds. You see that."

He hung up.

"For Christ's sake, hold the pool down a minute," he said.

The pay phone rang.

"Say Emergency Room," the guy said to Trotter. "Go ahead. Answer it. Say Emergency Room."

Trotter picked up the receiver and said, "Emergency Room."

"Well, *HORSESHIT*," one of the pool players yelled.

"This is Dr. Spock," Trotter said into the phone, winking at the guy. "That's right, your husband's here."

"Did I tell you, Ruth? Nobody's yelling horseshit. They're yelling Horskowitz. That's a doctor. Okay, Ruth. Okay, Ruth. I love you, too. Bye, Ruth."

The guy hung up again.

"A close one," the guy said to Trotter. "Thanks."

Trotter called Love of Gamblers Limited at home. Love had said there would be times when temptation would come walking out of the fog, looking like Miss Universe, in the raw, when it would be very hard, almost impossible, to resist the urge to gamble. When that happened, call me, Love said. Day or night. Love said he had seen it all and been through it all, and no matter how things looked, no matter how lucky you felt, no matter how good the tip was, no matter how handsome the dice felt, you've got to stand up to your sickness. You've got to be strong. You've got to praise the Lord. You've got to bring in the sheaves.

You've got to get serious.

Trotter had called Love at home once, after the second meeting of Gamblers Limited. Trotter had the overwhelming desire to bet "Monday Night Football." The home team always covered the number, it seemed, except when Trotter bet the home team. Trotter wanted to fake the football gods out by arranging a code with Lufkin so he would book the opposite of what Trotter said.

The football gods are kind of like Santa Claus, though. They can see under your bed and inside your brain.

Love talked Trotter down that time, gently, with information from charts and graphs, proving one game doth not a season maketh. So you luck the Monday night game out. The point is, over the long run, you can't win betting football because of the bookie's juice, or commission, the 10 per cent he gets for booking bets.

"Juice," is defined by Webster as that which the bookie squeezes from your body if you don't got no money.

Showboat Webster runs a bar down the street.

Love methodically explained to Trotter on the phone that night how betting football was like flipping coins with a guy, ten dollars a flip, but if you lost, you had to pay eleven dollars.

The number, the point-spread bookies put on a game makes it fifty-fifty, like flipping a coin.

Confronted with such a shocking display of reality, which gamblers would just as soon not mess with, Trotter agreed not to bet the Monday-nighter. He watched two minutes of the game as a neutral bystander. It was the dullest thing he had ever seen. Without gambling, things like the Giants would draw crowds of 130.

Trotter wanted to get some numbers from Love about how impossible it was to hit three winners in a row at the track. He wanted somebody to tell him to go home.

The phone at Love's house rang eight times and then a sobbing woman answered it. Trotter asked for Love.

"Not . . . here," the woman sniffed.

Trotter said it was VERY important. About an emergency. "Where can he be reached? It's critical."

"He's . . . oh, God . . . he's . . . at . . . the . . . the . . . RACE TRACK . . . he's . . ."

He's fallen off the old chariot, Trotter guessed.

"Listen," Trotter said to the woman, "maybe he's hot."

"You think?" she sniffed. "We could use the money."

Trotter hung up.

The phone rang quickly and Marty grabbed it and said, "Marty's."

He listened a moment. "Well there ARE some bodies here, but this isn't a lousy HOSPITAL. Hold on a second, lady."

Marty asked if there was a guy named Collins here, and if so, was he awake?

"Oh, no," Collins said. "Tell her I was kidnaped."

"He was kidnaped," Marty said into the phone. "Okay, I'll pass the message along." Marty put the phone back on the wall. "Collins, your wife says to knock real loud before you go in your apartment. She might have guests."

"Nice marriage," Marty said to Trotter.

"Made in heaven," Trotter nodded, finishing a beer.

"More like Taiwan," Marty said. "The way it seems to be falling apart."

THE BLOOD BANK IS SIX OR SEVEN BLOCKS UPHILL from the track, which works out for the best, since the guys are weak after giving, and can coast back.

Trotter got in his Buick and drove down over the curb and made a right.

Jake was not there.

Once the lot was full, and three hundred cars had been wedged into two hundred spaces, management was not responsible for hanging around.

A half a dozen guys were grouped by the front door of the blood bank, sobering up, because it would be a shame to give some poor blighter a transfusion of some wino's blood and have the recipient wake up roaring drunk.

The tour bus didn't stop here.

Neither did the buck. It went back to the track.

The going rate was about ten dollars a pint unless you had some rare type, in which case you could make as much as fifty dollars a bleeding.

It was pretty grim.

The volunteers were mostly old, wrinkled guys.

"Take a number," Trotter was told by a nurse.

"I don't want a malt or anything," he said. "I'm looking for a guy."

"Yeah, sure. Fill out this card. Have a seat."

"Is there a Looney here?"

"Mister," the nurse said. "Forget it. Fill the card in. It does not hurt to give blood. It will not take long. You are providing a valuable service. Do the card."

There were many stalls in the back. Trotter decided the only way he could see who was where—a donor's identity was carefully guarded—was to fill the damn card out.

He swore to God he had no horrible illnesses, and he signed the card. He had a seat next to an old rascal who said it was always crowded here when the favorites were coming in. "Let's go," he said to the nurse.

"You'll make the feature, easy," the nurse said. "Pipe down."

"What horses? I'm just anxious to serve my fellow man."

The old rascal winked at Trotter. By the looks of his arm, they might have to perform exploratory surgery to find any blood.

"Makes you a little dizzy is all," he told Trotter. "But hell, so does racing."

Men came and went.

So did a couple of women.

"Thirty-six," the nurse said.

Trotter got up and gave her his number and said, "Banana split."

He was led to a cubicle where a gorilla in a white smock with ROSEBUD tattooed on his forearm took Trotter's blood pressure.

"Am I all right?" Trotter asked.

"Beats me," the guy said.

"You work here?"

"When the blood starts flying, I come in and clean up, you know?"

"You just took my blood pressure."

"I did?"

Trotter was told to lie on his back.

"There's no money in my jacket," he said.

"I know," the guy said.

When the gorilla left, Trotter got up and sneaked down the hall, peeking in curtains, looking for Looney.

In the stall next to Trotter's, a *Racing Form* had been pinned to the curtain so an old boy could study the charts while he served mankind.

"Looney," Trotter said.

"Bird," somebody said from behind a curtain. "Do I win?"

"Looney!"

"What?"

Trotter opened some curtains.

It was not a pretty sight. His pal was on his back, giving blood. The jug was half full.

"Looney. What are you doing?"

"Being embalmed, if it's any of your business, which it isn't."

"Lufkin is looking for you."

"So?"

"He said you're over the limit."

"So? Dead men can't pay up."

"Don't go back to the track."

"I can't believe you screwed me."

"How, Looney? How'd I do that? I bet the horse we were both going to bet."

"I lost fifty dollars on that one named same as my cat. There's one named the same as my apartment in the seventh. I'm going back. I love it at the track. It's so wholesome. Great place to spend time with your friend. Until he sneaks off and screws you."

The nurse ran Trotter out.

"Give my regards to all your new friends in that whorehouse where you're sitting," Looney said.

Trotter told the receptionist he was chickening out and wanted to keep his blood. He was charged five dollars for the blood pressure check.

"I want to buy the guy's blood in the seventh booth."

"You can't do that. It goes to hospitals."

Trotter left an extra twenty. "Tell the guy his blood is extra-special. Tell him he gets thirty dollars instead of the regular ten."

"Ten?" the receptionist said. "His blood IS rare. He gets seventy-five dollars."

"In that case," Trotter decided. He put the twenty back in his shoe.

"What are you, some kind of vampire?" the old rascal by the door asked, as Trotter left.

Trotter missed the fourth race. It was run without incident, except only one horse won and eleven horses lost. The winner was named Rock Carrier and it paid six dollars.

Somebody should start a consulting firm to name horses for people with no imagination, Trotter decided.

He parked the Buick in the space he had vacated and beat it back to his box in the Jockey Club to await the arrival of his wife and treasurer.

Bernie Greenberg won on Rock Carrier. He also lost on the other eleven. He had bet twenty bucks on every damn horse there was in the fourth race—he said he forgot what a winner felt like.

"Oh really?" Miss Backstretch said.

"Winner HORSE, sweetie," he said.

Bernie had won sixty dollars on Rock Carrier, but he had lost two hundred and forty on the others, for a bottom line of minus one-eighty, but he said it was a moral victory.

"What's morals got to do with racing?" Miss Backstretch wondered.

The taste of victory, even one with an asterisk, agreed with Bernie Greenberg, so he bought some drinks for his friends and neighbors.

Trotter glanced at the *Racing Form* and noticed that there was a horse named Banana King entered and here he was drinking something foreign with bananas in it, but the message was not that strong.

There were only six horses entered in the fifth.

It was like a game show.

Do you pick what's behind one of the doors or do you pass?

Trotter knew what the audience would say:

Go for it!

"Where's the money?" Pam said.

She had been led to Trotter's table by a waiter, and the first thing she said was, "Where's the money?" rather loudly, Trotter thought. DAMN rather loudly.

"Who's THAT?" Miss Backstretch asked.

"This is Pam," Trotter said.

She took one look at Miss Backstretch's frontal attack and said, "We're married."

"This is Bernie," Miss Backstretch said. "We're not."

Trotter introduced his wife to Miss Backstretch.

"Backstretch? What kind of name is that?"

"British."

The early give-and-take did not go well, not at all.

When Pam went to the rest room, Miss Backstretch said, "She's pert. There's something to be said for pert, I guess."

She had quit trying to start a fire on Trotter's leg.

"We're not getting along at all," Trotter tried. He felt an ankle. "We almost hate each other."

That was worth a heel.

Pam didn't quite fit into the swim of things.

She wanted Trotter to give her the money for safekeeping which Trotter quietly informed her was impossible for thirty reasons.

First, the money was in his shoe. The second through the thirtieth reasons were the purse snatchers loitering outside the Jockey Club.

Pam had figured that the Trotters could make three rent and car payments with the money he had won, if it was *true*, that is, and she had made a list of other bills they could wipe from the face of the earth.

"What the hell good would that do?" he asked through gritted teeth. "We would be right back where we started in three months."

"Peace of mind," Pam said.

She asked that her husband give her all but ten dollars of his winnings. He could bet the ten on the next race, if he HAD to.

"Why can't you just sit here and watch the horses without betting?"

Trotter whispered that as there is no sound without ears, there can be no race without betting.

"That's poetic," Miss Backstretch said, overhearing.

"I'm not going to let you lose it all," Pam said.

"Be quiet, I beg you," Trotter said through smiling lips so nobody would know he and his wife were having a confrontation about money.

"If you don't give me the money, I'll make a scene."

"Okay," Trotter said.

"Okay what?"

Trotter whispered he would go to the bathroom and remove the money from his shoe. What he did, however, was go to the bar and have a drink, leaving his wife in the company of Bernie Greenberg and Miss Backstretch.

He asked about a double Wild Turkey and found out it was in season, so he legally killed it.

He removed the money from his shoe and walked to the fifty-dollar window. He placed it on the counter.

His old buddy the ticket seller made a noise through his teeth and said, "You're a champ. I mean it. You got more guts than you got sense. I love it."

"Thanks," Trotter said.

He felt a little like a gunfighter, standing there. A man has guts, you do what has to be done. You don't think about it. You DO it. It's a reflex.

"So what do you want?" the seller asked.

Trotter stood unblinking.

"I don't know," he said.

"It's a house rule, you have to give me a number."

"I'll be back."

"Believe me, I believe you."

TROTTER HALF-WALKED, HALF-STUMBLED DOWNSTAIRS and outside the main gate.

He took a survey before being discouraged by a cop.

He stopped fifteen people, three of whom refused to talk unless they received a gift.

He asked the people what they would do if they came to the races with fifty dollars and molded it into about twenty-four hundred, give or take a few rounds of drinks. Trotter told everybody he was working for a magazine. Some of the answers were very revealing.

Hugh McDermott, a truck driver, said, "That's ridiculous. There's nobody ever come with what you said and left with what you said. That's the dumbest thing I ever heard."

"Pretend," Trotter said. "Please."

"I would go home. I would *RUN* home. I would never come back. There's nobody in his right mind who would let it all ride. How come you're not taking notes?"

Trotter said he had a good memory.

Jack Vickers, an insurance salesman, said, "I'd take the winnings, no doubt about it. I'd take it and buy insurance, which is the greatest investment there is in this great country of ours."

Marie Glenn said, "You take another step and I'll spray you with Mace. It all depends on how much the person needed the money. You assume that anybody coming to the track with only fifty dollars would need the money a great deal. Therefore, my answer would be to leave with the money. Stay back, buddy."

Roger Minter, unemployed, said, "Loan me five."

Pete Call, a house painter, said, "Is this a joke? Not one person out of a thousand would bet it all. Not one out of ten thousand. When I get twenty bucks ahead, I come outside here and put it in an envelope and mail it home."

Roger Minter said, "Well then, loan me one."

Harry Valenti said, "If I was what you said up, I'd swallow all but two dollars. What kind of story are you writing?"

"Fiction," Trotter said.

All of the twelve people Trotter questioned said there was no doubt about it. The only logical move was right out the door.

That's what he figured.

Trotter went back inside the gate and conducted another hasty survey. The fifth race was still about fifteen minutes this side of history. There were only six horses scheduled for a six-furlong race. Trotter started asking people, "Who do you like?" This is a lot like asking somebody, "Do you have a good dentist?" Not many people are going to say, "No, the guy is a real amateur," even if he is, because you know what they say about misery.

It takes two to suffer.

If, for some ungodly reason the horse you like loses, if there is an earthquake or a 747 falls onto the backstretch, killing only your horse, then sometimes the only reason you can find for living is the knowledge that there are some guys out there just as sick as you. Misery loves surprise parties.

So if you tell somebody what horse you like, you have insurance.

You win, you've got a friend.

You lose, you've got a shoulder to cry on.

Nobody ever says, "MY dentist? He's got 20/200 vision for openers. And the shakes. You wouldn't want to go to MY dentist. He's bad."

Nobody ever says, either, "I don't know who is going to win," or, "You shouldn't want MY horse. He might lose."

What everybody says is, "Glad you asked."

Lackawanna Jones said, "I like the six horse for myriad reasons. Now the mostest reason I like the six horse is for numerology reasons. My name, it has got fifteen letters, counting the space, and one and five is six. I was born on six-six of '57. You add all that up and it is twenty-four, and two plus four is six. You can conclude six is the obvious choice."

Trotter had said, "Thanks."

Six was Duster.

Rake Smith said, "Four. You get this late in the season, you have to start betting trainers. Them jockeys is all alike. You get on a horse, there's only so much you can do, you know? It's what you do before the race that matters. It's the way you prepare them. Where you got similar horses, you get with the leading trainer, that's what. I met the trainer of the four horse, Millaway. The man could train a wasp. Everything you got goes on four."

Four was Moon Beam.

Lou Bagley said, "You kidding? You don't know already? I put everything I own on the one horse, and then some. A lot of people say, he's got the top weight, forget him. What he's also got is the post position. In

159

a short race, weight is about as important as an olive in a martini. The pressure is on, you can get by without, you follow me? Forget the weight. Weight is *NOTHING* in a six-furlong race. The post position is *EVERYTHING*. It's one. Wire to wire. I swear it."

One was Up Yours.

J. Donald McBright was sitting on a bench with a slide rule, a circular disc, a chart, a graph, a notebook, and colored pens. He had a killer headache. The pressure was on. J. Donald McBright was a Rhodes Scholar from Yale who had roomed with a guy named Lardass Fuller, who spent all his time making B-minuses and playing the horses. In a moment of supreme annoyance, when J. Donald McBright was studying for a math mid-term and Lardass Fuller was throwing darts at the Morning Line, J. Donald McBright issued the following statement, "Only an idiot does that." Lardass Fuller said, "Well J. Donald, if that's what you think, I have ten thousand that says you couldn't pick a winner, you dipshit."

Kids at Yale have a lot of money.

The bet was made and terms were arranged.

J. Donald McBright's father owned the left-hand corner of Maine. Lardass Fuller's father owned a used car lot.

Lardass Fuller gave J. Donald McBright one month—thirty days—to pick his winner, any horse, any race, any track.

J. Donald McBright had thrown himself into the project with such fervor, his over-all grade average dipped to 98 per cent. He came to the track every day, studying things. He invented a system based on net earnings, price/earnings ratios, speed ratings, humidity, and blinders, which are those things some horses wear so they can't see who the hell is passing them.

Lardass Fuller listened to J. Donald McBright and concluded the system was "Puke."

Lardass Fuller showed J. Donald the only system that works, darts.

This was the thirtieth day.

J. Donald McBright had wanted to make his selection for the first race, where Charity won, but a last-second cloud cover tilted his system, so he quickly went to work on his other preference, the fifth race.

Lardass Fuller had brought about fifty of his pals and they were drunk and giving J. Donald hell. One guy was counting off minutes and seconds until post time. Another guy was yelling out random numbers to confuse J. Donald.

When Trotter asked J. Donald McBright who he liked, J. Donald said, "Horse number two, I don't recall its name, I work only with numbers here; horse number two will win the race by four yards, two feet."

"Tell him why, J. Donald," Lardass Fuller said. "Tell him why you like two."

"The relationship of money won per race and the speed rating variance between the first and last eighths of the race," J. Donald McBright said. "Basically."

"The *REAL* reason is because he likes the color pink," Lardass Fuller said, spewing beer. "Two wears pink panties."

Lardass and his pals poured beer on each other as J. Donald McBright packed away his data and stalked confidently to the two-dollar window to put his money where his brains were.

The two horse was Rock It.

Glenda Robinson said, "Five."

Trotter asked, "Why?"

Glenda Robinson said, "I always bet on five."

Trotter said, "Oh."

Five was Idle Threat.

Jackson Mayberry said, "I like two, four, six, and one. Although five ain't that bad."

The people chose their horses for reasons like the jockey, the trainer, the condition of the track, the odds, the past performances, the law of averages, the hell of it, and some people even liked the HORSE.

The results of Trotter's little experiment were as follows:

If a person came with fifty dollars and somehow jacked it into twenty-four hundred dollars, he or she should, by all means, by ANY means, *GO HOME*.

If, however, he or she wanted to hang around the track awhile and soak up some atmosphere, bask in the glory, as it were, and since watching a horse for the beauty of it all was clearly impossible, if the big winner wanted to bet two small bucks on another race, just to keep his hand in it, you know, then the big winner should wager a pittance on one, two, four, five, or six, the cream of the fifth-race crop.

Nobody liked the three horse.

Horses one, two, four, five, and six were, five minutes before post time, listed anywhere between 2– and 8–1.

A tight one was in the offing.

Pick a horse to come in third.

Relax.

Have a drink.

Watch the girls.

Have a cigar.

Let the races be *FUN* for once.

"So three," Trotter said to his pal, the fifty-dollar ticket seller, whose name tag said he was Murdock.

"Three what?" Murdock asked.

"Three to win."

Murdock unclipped the program from his window and carefully looked from the three horse to the tote board.

"Here we go again," Murdock said to himself.

"You said it," Trotter agreed.

"I have a sneaky feeling you're going to bet all of that money on three to win. You ARE aware of what you're doing, of sound mind and all that?"

"You do wills?"

Murdock summoned one of his supervisors to witness this substantial transaction. When you got up in the thousands, the track was very careful. The supervisor inspected a couple of the hundred-dollar bills.

"They're yours," Trotter said.

"Now," Murdock said carefully. "You want win tickets on the three horse in the fifth race, is that right?"

"Yes," Trotter nodded positively. "Right. Perfect."

A crowd had gathered behind the action.

Murdock counted the money. It came to twenty-four hundred dollars. Fifty divided into that is forty-eight. "You get back forty-eight win tickets on the three horse in the fifth race. Don't you want to KEEP any money back, um, kind of, in case?"

"In case what?"

"In case you get thirsty or hungry before the race is over?"

Trotter dipped into his right front pocket and came up with a dollar and a half in change. "I'm fine."

"Okay," Murdock said. "Here we go."

Ka-chunk, forty-eight times.

Murdock wrapped all the win tickets in a rubber band and handed them to Trotter.

There was a smattering of applause from the rear.

Murdock's supervisor snapped his fingers and an armed track security man hustled up. The cop was to

163

escort Trotter to his seat, and if necessary, stay with him during the race.

"I do this for a living," Murdock the ticket seller said. "Been doing it sixteen years. We make the circuit, you know? One track closes, another opens. Here, Arkansas, Nebraska, Kentucky, the Coast. Some big places, some dumps. I've met all kinds of characters. Let me tell you though, pal, you're the champ. I hope you win."

"I'd tip you except all I have is six quarters."

"God bless," Murdock said. "I mean it. You're the all-time indoor champ. You're the greatest I ever saw. I'm going to tell my grandkids about you. You're something."

"Well," Trotter said.

Pam didn't take it so well.

She thought Trotter had been arrested, with that cop leading him in.

"Where's the money?" she asked.

"Gone by-by," Trotter said weakly.

He spread the forty-eight win tickets on the table.

He had planned to say something noble, like how he was doing it for them, like how peace of mind should last more than three rotten months, like how this substantial wager would be a true test of their love.

Instead he shrugged and said, "Ah, piss on it."

"I can't believe it," Pam said. "I can *NOT* believe it."

She got up.

"I had to," Trotter said.

"You should have your head examined," she said.

"Lay off him," Miss Backstretch said. She glanced at the tote board to check three's odds, then said, "Although the bet was a little weird. *NOBODY* hardly likes three."

"Precisely," Trotter said. He had a double.

164

"Everybody would quit, as far ahead as you were," Pam said.

"Again, precisely."

"We could have used the money."

"I could use a drink."

"You're seriously ill," Pam said. "And you're driving me crazy. I'm sick to my stomach. I'm going home."

"Good," Miss Backstretch said.

"Should I call if I win?" Trotter asked his wife.

She didn't say no.

The size of Trotter's bet was not that unique within the confines of the Jockey Club. God knows, more money had been bet. More money might even have been *tipped*. But it was a hearty bet, nevertheless, and the bet, combined with the *NEED* and the domestic drama that had unfolded as Pam folded up her tent and left her husband babbling incoherently, well, that got everybody's attention. What *REALLY* got their attention was the tote board, where the odds on Trotter's selection, the three horse.

It was 26–1.

Trotter's unexpected and noteworthy bet had knocked the odds down from about 40.

"You're looking at sixty-nine grand," Bernie Greenberg said. "Or you're looking at nothing."

Quite a few big shots, hearing of Trotter's bet, wandered by to wish him luck. None of them, though, voiced any redeeming social value in the horse of Trotter's choice.

It was just a horse.

It was named Fleet Dreams, which was a pretty lousy name.

Its parents were Wet Fleet and Big Dreams, so it could have been worse.

"I was wondering if you might like to spend a

weekend at my townhouse in Vermont," the woman with a tweed hat, jacket, and slacks said. "I like men with guts."

"He's mine," Miss Backstretch said. Bernie had wandered off to bet.

Trotter spread apart the win tickets, had a drink of whiskey, and fanned himself.

THE BLOUSE WENT.

It happened so suddenly.

The button shot forward and bounced off the glass with such force it landed three tables behind Trotter's.

There was a scramble for the souvenir.

There was also a scramble to assist Miss Backstretch, who handled the outburst with aplomb, all things considered. Two of the things you *HAD* to consider were her breasts.

The blouse flew open like a curtain being drawn from the middle. It flapped around her ribs. She had nice ribs.

Miss Backstretch was wearing a bra or they would have had to call out the fire department. When you got right down to it, and several waiters tried, you could have probably come up with a better word than "bra" for what Miss Backstretch was wearing under her dearly departed blouse. It, whatever it was, was flesh-colored and seemingly made of cobwebs. At first glance, it looked like skin, but upon glances two through ten, you could see it was material.

There were many material witnesses.

One gentleman three boxes up the finish line leaned forward for a better look and fell over the rail and hit his bald head on the glass.

"Well hell," Miss Backstretch said. She pulled the

right part of her blouse over the flesh-colored body stocking.

Trotter was faced with the most difficult decision of his life.

His horse, Fleet Dreams, was in a battle for the lead at the top of the stretch when the button blew. That was what had caused Miss Backstretch to scream at the top of her, you know, lungs, *"COME ON BABY!"* Fleet Dreams had come from dog-last to challenge for first. Everybody in the area was cheering for Trotter. The follow-through of Miss Backstretch's cheer, where she exhaled with such power, uprooted the button.

Trotter felt responsible.

To his left was the horse that could win him peace of mind, financial security, and maybe even a write-up in the *National Enquirer*. To his right was Miss Backstretch, her breasts standing at attention beneath the body stocking-thing. It was a difficult decision, what to watch.

He chose right.

It was a compliment Miss Backstretch would not forget, having a guy think your breasts are better-looking than sixty-nine thousand dollars.

He chose right partly because Miss Backstretch was a nice-looking woman and partly because he was too feeble to watch his horse. When Fleet Dreams had made its move turning for home, Trotter's teeth began chattering and there were white caps in his stomach. He felt faint. He felt insane.

There was screaming in the Jockey Club.

Trotter had become the mascot of the ladies and gentlemen who bob for olives. They thought he was quaint. When Mrs. Van Slyke was informed by her son there was a character down the way who had bet his life savings on a long shot, she put her cat down and stood on a chair for a look at the finish.

Mrs. Van Slyke's cat is smuggled into the Jockey Club up the dumb-waiter by a waiter named Buck, who is handsomely rewarded with a fifty. Buck the waiter then handsomely rewards the captain of the Jockey Club with a twenty. When the president of the track is in attendance, the captain of the Jockey Club takes Mrs Van Slyke's cat and gives a guy ten to walk it outside. Cats are against the rules.

Mrs. Van Slyke admired the pioneering spirit in the earthy gentleman down the way who bet all he had on the long shot, so before the race, she sent a twenty along with a waiter with her best wishes, which Trotter accepted without batting an eye.

The note with the twenty had read:

I wish I had your balls.

Sincerely, Doris Van Slyke, widow.

When Trotter glanced up the way, a woman had tipped her opera glasses.

Even the waiters showed interest in the finish of this particular race. Usually, they regarded a race with all the emotion of a young surgeon who was working on commission.

Trotter was the only person who didn't react one way or another at the finish.

He concluded the race was over when Miss Backstretch left her chair like she was coming out of a cake at a Shriners' convention. She lunged across the table and grabbed Trotter by the neck and fell on top of him. They both fell over backward.

"Did I win?" he asked.

She planted a big kiss on his lips. It grew into another.

Bernie Greenberg said, "Hey, that's about enough of that."

Believe it or not, he won.

He won roughly sixty-nine thousand dollars.

Trotter was so happy, it wasn't happiness, it was beyond that, it was *HEAVEN*; he banged his fists on the table and knocked over a few drinks and broke a candle holder, for which he was charged. A waiter named Harvey brought Trotter a bill, hell, it wasn't five minutes after he busted the candle thing—it was about *TWO* minutes—and the bill was for $120.20.

"It was Waterford crystal, sir," Harvey said, holding the bill like he was a traffic cop.

"What the hell is *THIS*?" Trotter asked. His head was dizzy. His eyes were red.

"A bill, sir."

Trotter told Harvey what he could do with the bill, which was wrap the broken candle holder in it, and then some.

Trotter was almost in shock with the victory.

His language was the subject of several remarks like, "They should put a guard on the back door so rude people can't sneak in."

"That's ten for the trousers," Bernie Greenberg said.

Bernie Greenberg presented Trotter with a dry-cleaning tab.

Bernie had taken his lady by the wrist and he had jerked her back beside him with the instructions, "Get that damn blouse fixed, damn it."

"Okay, Bernie," Miss Backstretch said. She pinned it together with a safety pin.

Trotter wondered briefly why nobody was congratulating him.

Bernie Greenberg angrily tore his tickets in half and threw them in the air. The pieces settled on Trotter.

"Thanks for the ticker-tape parade," he said.

"You might have mentioned," Bernie Greenberg said.

"What?"

"The three horse. You might have mentioned you liked him, for Christ's sake. You think I couldn't have used it?"

Trotter started to explain the path that led him to the three horse, which was the sidewalk out front, but then, nobody would have believed him, and, more importantly, it was nobody's business.

"I hate people that sneak around and bet," Bernie said. "I knew a kid in school that kept all his answers covered like a little sissy."

Trotter was feeling too good to get in an argument. He ordered a fast drink.

One of the women in tweed said something that ended with "can't hold his liquor."

Being without funds until he collected, Trotter put his next drink on Mastercharge, and when the card was late getting back, Trotter accused the waiter, Harvey, of possible graft.

"I assure you, sir, we're quite busy," Harvey said.

Trotter told Harvey of a game a guy named Mulligan used to work in a fancy restaurant. Mulligan was a waiter, too. A customer named Roberts came in with a big party for dinner and gave his American Express to Mulligan. Well, fifteen minutes later, the customer Roberts said to the waiter Mulligan, "Where is my card?"

"Sir, we're busy," Mulligan said.

What had happened was Mulligan gave the American Express to a friend of his out in the alley behind the kitchen, and Mulligan's friend ran across the street and fast-charged four steel-belted radials on Roberts' American Express.

When it was all over, Mulligan brought the American Express card back to Roberts to sign for the dinner, apologizing for the slight delay, and in addition to radials, Mulligan got a good tip. When the bill for the tires came in, a month or so later, Roberts probably didn't know what hit him. Mulligan worked the credit card blitz many, many times, until he tried to work it twice on the same person, and was arrested.

"So I want my damn Mastercharge in one minute," Trotter told Harvey.

Harvey was humiliated.

"Here's to all you stuffy bastards," Trotter toasted, before leaving to collect his fortune.

The way it works in the Jockey Club is:

You don't keep secret horses from those at your table. That's rude.

When you win, you don't begin swearing and screaming and knocking over Waterford crystal and whiskey.

You don't flirt with another's lady.

When you win, a nod of the head will do.

You don't come in here out of the blue and make a jackass out of yourself by winning an enormous amount of money. The plan is, you try to break even. If you start winning enormous sums of money, then that will take all the fun out of racing. People will try to *MAKE* money instead of trying to pick up girls or figure which flute was off key at the opera last night, or talk stocks or bonds. You wander in here off the street and win a lot of money, then people might concentrate on winning money instead of dressing proper, and there goes the neighborhood.

In sum, the way it works in the Jockey Club is:

Nobody loves a winner.

Losing is a status symbol.

Trotter hired a guard for a hundred dollars an hour after leaving the Jockey Club with a bad taste in his mouth. The guard was a cop who just got off traffic duty out front. Trotter had gone to the track manager's office for advice.

The guard was in uniform, which helped. The guard walked with his right hand on his pistol. It would take a real fool to attempt a robbery under such circumstances. Now if only the cop didn't rob Trotter, he would have it made.

The cop's name was Reardon.

He was a kid of about twenty-five.

"Don't worry about a thing," Reardon said.

"Anybody makes a funny move, shoot them on sight," Trotter said.

Reardon almost shot a guy wearing a handle-bar mustache who ran out of the crowd as Trotter was standing in line to collect his money. The handlebar mustache screamed, "Trotter!"

Reardon unfastened his holster and grabbed the gun butt.

Looney ripped off the false mustache and Trotter said, "It's okay, I know this guy."

The second Looney ripped off his false mustache, Lufkin's man, Johnny Casino, who was *ALSO* disguised, he was in a beard, grabbed Looney and said, "Pay up you deadbeat."

Reardon didn't know who to shoot, or why.

Trotter said he hadn't *collected* yet, there was no reason to shoot anybody.

"What's going on here, anyway?" Reardon wondered. He was a little irritated. *Thinking* wasn't part of the deal. A man signs on to guard some cash, he guards some cash. Nobody said he was going to be called on to figure who to shoot. "What's all these men ripping off disguises for?"

It was, Trotter had to admit, a little hard to explain.

Johnny Casino had Looney's elbow and Looney had Trotter's elbow. Reardon had backed off, with his legs apart, in case he had to draw down on one of these fruitcakes.

The pitiful one, Looney, owed the other one, the dangerous one, some money, was about the size of it.

Johnny Casino's right eyelid was twitching. He reminded Trotter of a rattler about to strike.

"I don't like you one fuck," Johnny Casino said to Trotter. "A man makes fun of my shoes, he makes fun of me."

Johnny had changed to brown shoes that looked like they had once been a part of a shag carpet.

"If I hear another utterance of profanity," Reardon said to Johnny, "I'm gonna blast your head off."

"Oh really?"

"That's correct."

"I lost the money," Looney said. "The blood money—from the blood bank."

Trotter said he was not surprised.

"No, not that," Looney said. "Not on a horse. Lost it, lost it. *REALLY* lost it. The only thing I can guess is my pocket was picked while I was going to the bathroom. Somebody must have reached under one of those stalls and gone through my back pocket."

"You hear anybody say, Bless you?"

"As a matter of fact, yeah."

Reardon said that narrowed it down, but he still made a note. He said there were only approximately thirty-two people floating around here disguised as priests, or whatever you call them.

"You mean my pocket was picked by a priest?" Looney asked. "That's about the last straw. He got seventy-five bucks."

Reardon said that pocket-picking in the john was the latest rage among the criminal element. A guy's pants are just real vulnerable.

"Nothing is sacred," Looney said.

"What is all this?" Johnny Casino said. "Social hour? Come on, you greasy little bastard, you deadbeat. You owe us and I plan to by God get it."

"Okay, that does it," Reardon said. He removed his walkie-talkie from his belt and identified himself and requested an on-duty cop at sector B-3, by the second-level fifty-dollar window. "You're under arrest, punk."

Johnny Casino's entire face began twitching. It looked like he was a puppet, and somebody was warming up on the face strings. His eyes, lips, and jaws jerked without rhyme or reason.

"Now wait," Trotter said.

"Arrest him, go on," Looney said. He almost smiled.

"Swearing in public," Reardon said.

"You dirty..." Johnny almost said.

"Yes?" Reardon asked.

Johnny said, "Bastard is no swear. It's some kind of dog. That's no swearing. Neither is son of a bitch, you son of a bitch."

Trotter said, "Wait a minute, Reardon. He knows Frank Sinatra."

"So?"

The mere mention of Sinatra had a neutralizing effect on Johnny Casino. Word was, Sinatra thought things over and decided being banished from Vegas was not punishment enough for Johnny. Word was, Sinatra was still pissed, being called a deadbeat.

"Let the three of us talk this over," Trotter told Reardon.

"Don't call Sinatra," Johnny said to Trotter. "Please. He don't know where I am. He'll feed me to a sea bass."

"Looney owes you how much?"

"Eight hundred and fifty."

"Can you believe I bet five hundred dollars on the

174

Giants? I can't believe it. There I was at the phone at Marty's, going to bet fifty dollars. The next thing I knew, I was saying, give me five hundred. It was like, Trotter, somebody else saying it, making the bet, like a strange force. Let him kill me. I deserve to die, betting so much on those people."

"Here's the plan, Johnny. I'll cover for Looney. I won some money here, so when I get it, I'll cover, pay his tab."

Johnny shrugged. "Money is money." He removed his book and turned to Looney's page.

"Listen, when's the last time I had a winning week, look it up," Looney said.

Johnny thumbed back and back and back. "December 5, three years ago."

"My God. That's a long time."

"You win, let's see, you hit three out of five basketballs that week, and three out of six footballs, let's see, you're in the black that week, you win that week, um, twenty-two bucks."

"Well for the love of God."

"So when I collect here, we'll settle Looney's sheet, okay?"

"Okay by me."

"Oh, Trotter," Looney said. "You don't need to do that. I'll get the money. I'll kill somebody, I can get it."

"What?" Reardon said from off to the side. "What was that?"

"Nothing," Trotter said.

He told Looney it was all right, he had won quite a bit. What were friends for, anyway?

Looney stepped forward and embraced Trotter. "I'm committed to you for the rest of my life," Looney said solemnly. "I will serve you forever. You're the greatest man that ever lived, and I mean that."

Trotter also volunteered to pay Johnny Casino's

175

fine for swearing in public, which came to twenty dollars. Trotter gave an IOU to Reardon.

"Get a receipt," Johnny said.

"The secret of modern law enforcement," Reardon said so Johnny Casino could hear, "is eliminating the punks at the grass-roots level. You let cheap punks buffalo a member of the legal community, you're in trouble."

Johnny put his hand over his heart, where there had to be one or more weapons, and Trotter calmed things by whistling, "That's life, that's what all the people say. Riding high in April, shot down in May," and the double meaning put the fear of God back in Johnny Casino, and he put his hands in his pockets.

Getting paid, this time, was like the changing of the Palace Guard. It was a very formal, no-nonsense event. When Trotter placed his win tickets on the counter, the cashier pressed a buzzer and a man in a pin-striped suit arrived to verify that these were bona fide win tickets and not forgeries.

Reardon stood with his back to the proceedings and the window, watching for trouble.

"Congratulations, sir," the track official in the pin-striped suit said. "You are a very big winner, indeed."

"I know," Trotter said.

The man in the pin-striped suit spoke with track security guards. An adding machine was produced and the amount of Trotter's winnings was double-, triple-, and quadruple-checked.

Murdock, who had sold Trotter the tickets, was standing behind the window. "I know that man," he said. Trotter waved.

It came to sixty-nine thousand dollars and some change, which the man in the pin-striped suit said was "very unusual."

Trotter did not know about that.

This amount of money was not kept at the windows, so it had to be sent for—will five-hundreds be all right? the man in the pin-stripe suit wondered. The track official said that he had worked here eighteen years, and Trotter's win was the fourth most he had ever seen won on a single race.

"Two weeks ago, an Arab bet a hundred thousand on the favorite to show, and it paid something like eighty thousand. But sir, in all the years I've been here, yours is the most won on such an, if I may take the liberty of saying so, unusual bet. Not many people gave Fleet Dreams much of a chance. You should be very proud."

"Proud's behind," Trotter said. "Where's my money?"

"You going to let it ride?" Murdock asked. "I say he lets it ride. The man has the guts of a burglar."

"You watch it," Reardon said.

Let it ride?

It was a possibility Trotter hadn't considered. Letting it ride would probably be criminal. You don't let something like peace' of mind ride. You don't *BET* happiness. Now, it's true, nothing is nothing. If you go home with nothing, it doesn't matter if you HAD BEEN up to $6.90 or $69,000. But on the other hand, chickening out on a hot streak was about as low-brow as you could get. What Trotter needed was a sign, a vibe, that gave some indication that the hot streak was about to peter out.

Trotter filled out the tax form as he awaited the arrival of one hundred and thirty-eight five-hundred-dollar bills.

He sent five bottles of champagne to Fleet Dreams's stall, roses to the owner, and a case of low-calorie beer to the jockey.

He had his picture taken with the pin-striped suit,

the seller, Murdock, and the cashier of record, a guy named Mosley. When somebody makes a big score, it's great publicity, like when a woman from Des Moines wins a hundred thousand on the dollar slot machine in Vegas. A big win gives the masses the impression it *CAN* be done, which it can, but the thing is, you don't see many stories about the women from Seattle, and the men from New Orleans, and the men and women from Tulsa who pour hundreds of thousands of silver dollars in those machines without receiving so much as a "Thank you" in return. There's not going to be a story about Looney, bleeding away his last fifty dollars on a horse named for his cat. That is as much a human interest story as Trotter's.

So whereas you might think The Track would be in a foul mood coughing up a big pay-off, and whereas you might think it would prefer suppressing news of a score, you're wrong. There are approximately hundreds of thousands, maybe millions, of guys just like Trotter *WAS*, out there, and if they think a big win is possible, to each his own. So be it. It is *NOT* possible to bet $2,300 on a 30–1 shot and win.

At least, it's highly unlikely.

The fact that Trotter *DID* the impossible means, if you want to analyze things, as the old man in the pin-striped suit probably already had in his head, that nobody will bet $2,400 on a 26–1 shot and win for something like 2,400 more years.

The bottom line is, Trotter was good for business.

It wasn't the track's money, anyway. The sixty-nine grand came from the dummies who had bet the favorites in the fifth race. The track gets its percentage, regardless. So what really happened was that Trotter got into the drawers of many innocent men and women who bet the favorites. But a success story brings people to the track, and the more money bet, the more the track earns from its God-given cut.

"Five, one thousand; five, two thousand; five, three; five, four; five, five thousand," the cashier counted.

Peace of mind is a wonderful thing, Trotter concluded.

God, the government must sleep great, with all the pieces of peace of mind it gets.

"Five, ten thousand; five, eleven."

Trotter figured the government would confiscate half of the sixty-nine grand, leaving what? thirty-four five?

He owed eight on the Buick, leaving twenty-six five, and five and a half on a furniture loan, leaving twenty-one, and Pam had her eye on a goddamn water cruise that was four, leaving seventeen, and he could pay the rent four—no, three, years, for twelve even, leaving a total of five fucking thousand dollars!

"Hell, I'm broke," Trotter said.

"Huh?" Reardon said.

"Five, twenty; five, twenty-one; five, twenty-two."

Not even five thousand.

The champagne he sent to the owners of Fleet Dreams was two hundred, and the roses were fifty, and the beer was ten, and the broken glass in the Jockey Club was, hell, a hundred something, and Looney's tab was almost nine hundred, and Johnny Casino's fine was twenty, and all that, hell, that came to one thousand, two hundred and some bucks.

"Five, fifty; five, fifty-one."

Trotter was only ahead about $3,800! After the big win!

"Looney, there's some bad news about the money," Trotter said. He was going to say he needed to keep it.

"I love you," Looney said. "There is all kinds of

179

love. Lover love. Brother love. Mate love. Man love. I love you, man to man, friend to friend."

"Watch it," Reardon said.

"Five, sixty; five, sixty-one."

"About the eight hundred or so you owe," Trotter said.

"You're a prince. A king."

"Oh hell."

"What about it?"

"Here."

Trotter gave Looney two five-hundreds, and Looney gave them to Johnny Casino.

"You'll be back," Johnny said to Looney.

"Not me," Looney said. "I have seen the light."

"Excuse me," Trotter said. "I hate to interrupt, but somebody owes me some change."

Johnny Casino and Looney said, together, "Oh. Yeah."

Johnny gave the C-note and change to Looney, who gave it to Trotter.

"Sixty-eight, five; SIXTY-NINE even. Congratulations, sir."

Reardon requested and received a metal box. The money was placed there. "Where to?" Reardon asked.

"Good question," Trotter said.

As Trotter thought about a good place to store sixty-nine thousand dollars, the track official in the pin-stripe suit said, "Pardon me, Mr. Trotter."

"Yeah?"

"*Continued* good luck."

THAT was subliminal advertising if Trotter had ever not seen it.

THE PROCESSION PICKED UP SOME NEW MEMBERS AND swept toward the Jockey Club.

Reardon had the money box in his left hand. His right rested on the gun.

Looney brought up the flank, like a faithful puppy.

Evangeline had made a run to a branch bank for a couple of hundred and she read the *Racing Form* with grim determination as she and Sid Booten walked with Trotter.

"If we blow this, Sid," she said positively of the two hundred, "I'll take the braces off myself."

Sid said he thought he had found a sleeper in the next race.

Evangeline looked up the horse in the *Form* and said, "Sid, for once today, you're right. That horse is a definite sleeper. Only I wish you would start picking horses that didn't *RUN* in their sleep. Sid, you've got to get serious, here."

"Yes, honey," Sid said.

Reardon almost gut-shot Tony Cheeseburger. Reardon had his holster unsnapped before Trotter could say, "It's all right."

Tony caught his breath and said, "I *KNOW* that guy. Who you like in the feature, Trotter?"

"That guy is a punk," Reardon said to Trotter, snapping his holster back shut. "He'd sell his sister to gypsies for ten bucks."

"Make it twenty," Tony said.

Reardon said Tony used to walk back and forth across the street in front of the track, waiting for a car to come close, then he would fake being hit.

Trotter didn't know who he liked in the feature, or if he even *liked* the feature.

Trotter and his party were refused entry to the Jockey Club. Since he left to collect, it seemed, several new rules were being enforced.

No loaded pistols were permitted.

No guests were permitted.

No punks were permitted.

"Listen, Marty's got a safe if you want to leave your money there," Looney said.

It was true. That's where he aged the grilled cheeses.

"Come back, sir," the man on the door of the Jockey Club said, "when, um, it's... proper."

Trotter sniffed and followed Reardon to the stairs.

Looney hung behind and said, "Excuse me," to the man on the door. He leaned inside and yelled, "Hey, you phonies."

Everybody turned around.

Looney nodded and said, "See what I mean?"

Nobody in Marty's knew exactly what to make of Trotter yet. It was true, there wasn't much to talk to him about because he had won an ungodly amount of money, but on the other hand, he had won so *MUCH*, you couldn't help but respect the guy.

Reardon knew EXACTLY what to make of those in Marty's.

He removed his gun and placed it on the table.

"I want your attention," he said. "I have an announcement. Anybody coming within fifteen yards of this table without clearance is going to get his kneecaps shot off. That's all."

Trotter threw common sense to the wind and bought a round for the house, plunging him further toward debt. There were only eight guys and one honorary guy, Evangeline, in there, so nine beers was only five bucks or so.

"Make it ten," Marty said. "*I'M* in the house."

"Well, well, look who's honoring us with a visit." Vibes Eberhart was massaging his temples. The visions were obviously few and far apart.

182

"He bought you a beer," Looney said. "You could at least thank him."

"Who the hell are you, his nanny?"

"How're things in the great beyond?" Trotter asked.

"There's icicles hanging on all the letters," Eberhart said.

"That must mean bet hockey," Trotter said.

"Who knows. There's still time. I just can't get rid of this blistering headache."

"There's one in the next race named Fast Relief," Looney said.

"What's that got to do with anything? Fast Relief? I get it. Fast relief relieves a headache. Is that right? Is that what you mean, Looney? That's not bad. It's not great. But it's pretty good. It might be a Back Door Vibe, which I get once in a while, but don't usually figure it out until after the fact. Looney, I might buy you a beer."

"I might thank you," Looney said.

Sid Booten found what he thought was a horse for the sixth race, but Evangeline discarded it with a brush of her hand and asked Sid please to clam up and let her think.

"Want another beer?" Sid asked. "It's good for your hair. It's true."

"That's the dumbest thing I ever heard," Looney said. "Beer's good when you *WASH* your hair in it, not drink it."

"It's the same premise," Sid Booten said.

"Will you people please be quiet so I can think," Evangeline asked.

Nobody could put his finger on the atmosphere in Marty's. Trotter had, somehow changed. Marty noticed it first. Trotter had walked in the place kind of cold and removed. He had bought a round for the house without bitching, which isn't normal. He hadn't touched his beer. If a person wants to win an impossible sum of money and move into a new bracket of friends, that's his business. Even though Trotter had said he felt fine, normal, the change in his personality was confirmed when Marty said, "Anybody for lunch? The grilled cheeses will be done any day now."

"That's a good idea," Trotter said. "Another round, first though. A martini for me." Trotter pushed his beer to Reardon.

Reardon was staring at the front door, but had matters under control with his peripheral vision. "It's a gift. I can see my ears."

"That's because you've got enormous ones," Vibes Eberhart said.

"Don't shoot him," Trotter said.

"So that's your fortune," Sid Booten said, nodding at the metal box on the table. "So that's sixty-nine thousand dollars."

"Buddy, I don't want to hear you mention that box again," Reardon said.

The request for a martini had knocked the wind out of Marty, but he was like a camel in that regard, and had reserves, and he recovered to say, "A *what*?"

"Martini."

"I've heard of those," Marty said. "What's in it?"

"Vodka or gin," Trotter said.

"Oh yeah. Right. Most people call them gins or vodkas, though."

"*AND* vermouth."

"Oh. Right."

"And an olive."

"I got the olives stuck on the sandwiches."

"You mind if we drink beer at this table?" Vibes Eberhart asked. "Or should we go in the crapper?"

Everybody watched Trotter sample the cheese

martini. The olive had grilled cheese wrapped around its edges. It was like he was taking a sip of something that would grow fur on his hands and fangs in his mouth.

Trotter said it was not bad.

"You want another one?"

"Yeah," Trotter said, "and the house phone."

"That does it," Vibes Eberhart said. "I'm changing tables."

Marty didn't know what to make of Trotter's request at first, but then when it became obvious that Trotter wasn't making a joke, when Trotter *again* asked that the house phone please be brought to his table, Marty said, "This is not a house. This is a bar. The pay phone is over on the wall, same as the last, what, two or three decades?"

"Let me go rip it out of the wall for *MISTER* Trotter," Vibes said, collecting his beer as he got up to change tables.

"Keep your hands where I can see them," Reardon said. "And move slow and easy."

"Oh yeah," Trotter said. "The wall."

He got up and left Reardon guarding the money box and placed a call and what happened because of this call, about twenty minutes later, was the damnedest thing ever seen in Marty's since he hired a guy named Cronkite to paint Citation's picture over the bar. Cronkite was all the time falling off the scaffold, into the sink. What happened because of Trotter's call provided material for more discussion since the time Earless Tom Beck was found dead of suicide in the trunk of his car with a coat hanger wrapped around his neck.

In twenty minutes there was a knock on Marty's front door.

Nobody usually knocked.

The Health Department was on the prowl or

somebody new was outside. Marty went to the door and let in three short Chinese gentlemen who nodded gracefully and said they were looking for Mr. Trotter.

"Over here," Trotter said. "It's okay, Marty."

The three Chinese gentlemen walked to Trotter's table.

"Ro," the leader said.

This means hello.

An elegant meal was spread in front of Trotter, a mini-buffet, shrimp roll, egg roll, chicken, beef, pork. The Chinese gentlemen shoved three tables together. "You better eat this quick," one of them said, waving his hand at the smoke, "or it'll taste like cigarette butts."

"Hear you creaned up," another said. His name tag was Flank. "Really," the guy said. "It's Flank. How much you win? Hopefully enough to pay for this, you know?"

The bill was for seventy-five dollars, which Trotter requested from Reardon.

Reardon had the Chinese gents back off before removing a C-note from the box.

"Keep it," Trotter said of the tip.

"You okay guy," Flank said. "Come back, you understand?"

Marty couldn't believe his eyes. "I've been in this business a long time and this is the most chickenshit thing I've ever seen. It's worse than stealing. Happy Hour is hereby canceled the rest of the month."

"Help yourself," Trotter said of the food.

"Now just a damn minute. This is no campground." Marty stood with his arms folded. The guys (and Evangeline) looked from Marty to the plates of steaming food.

"You'll get over it," Evangeline said to Marty. She

took a miniature drumstick and had a bite.

"It's nothing personal," Looney said, lumping shrimp rolls on a paper plate.

"A round of rice wine," Trotter said to Marty.

"Is that a joke?"

"Yes."

Several people had wandered in, so the round Trotter bought was a little more worthwhile. "The grilled cheese just went down a nickel and the beer just went up a nickel."

One of those who had wandered in was Jake, the guy who could stop a car on a dime and park a car on a half-dollar. Trotter had been thinking about Jake and the Buick. Trotter waved Jake over.

"Hey," Jake said. "Sanders! How's the chicken business?"

"That's close enough," Reardon said.

Trotter said he was okay, too.

"You know a strange assortment of people," Reardon said. "What's that punk talking about, chicken business?"

"Inside joke."

"Joke, what joke?" Jake adjusted the bill of his ball cap and sat down. He was already puzzled.

"Listen," Trotter said, "I've been thinking."

"You gonna give me something else? I like motorcycles."

"You know the Buick?"

"Do I *KNOW* it? I *LOVE* it."

"Now listen, Jake. I've won some money today. I think I really might give you the Buick. If today turns out all right, it's yours. I was worrying about that. It's only fair."

"What? Give. You already did that. What is this?"

"I owe about seventy-nine hundred on it."

187

"Owe what? What?"

"I might not be able to afford to give you that car, Jake. I feel bad about it. If I can't give it to you, hell, I don't know what to say."

Jake removed the ball cap and scratched his head. "Now just a damn minute here. You're not Lieutenant Sanders?"

"Here's what, Jake. How about I give you a hundred bucks right now, mental anguish. Okay?"

"What was that business about giving me the car?"

Looney said so they could get a parking spot on the front row.

"I'll still give you the car," Trotter said. "If you want."

"And you owe seventy-nine, is that what you're saying?"

Trotter nodded.

"You'll give me the car you owe seventy-nine on, or you'll give me a hundred-dollar bill?"

"Right now, that's the best I can do."

"You give your car away earlier?" Looney asked.

"Yeah," Jake said. "But it was only worth sixty bucks."

"So you can clear forty," Looney said.

"But I lost thirty-five on the horses."

"Five dollars is five dollars," Looney decided.

"Here's two hundred," Trotter said, nodding to Reardon.

"I don't believe this," Vibes Eberhart said.

Jake folded the money and put it in his shirt pocket. He said it was not exactly what he had in mind and that at this moment he had absolutely no faith in the human race. Vibes Eberhart had to agree with Marty. This whole scenario reeked of bullshit.

"That's no way to talk to a winner," Looney said. "A saint."

A winner. That had a nice ring to it.

"So what do you want me to do with this, um," Reardon lowered his voice, "box of assets?"

"Safe rental is twenty bucks," Marty said.

"Attaboy, Marty," Vibes said.

Trotter said, "That's a good question. Just keep an eye on it there, Reardon, for a second."

"I have perfect peripheral vision. There is now a man throwing up by the pool table to the left. Two men are asleep on the table to the right, by the door to the john. One of the bulbs is burned out overhead. There is a fly on the money box."

Reardon definitely had a grip on things.

A GUY NAMED TOMPKINS RAN IN THE FRONT DOOR with news of the sixth race, which was now official.

"Who?" Marty asked. He puts the winner and pay-off on the blackboard.

"Fast Relief, by two lengths, Run Gunner and B B Gunn," Tompkins said. "The winner pays twelve, seven, and five."

"God bless America!" Vibes Eberhart said, slamming his fist on the table. He put his head in his hands and drifted off into oblivion or meditation for the seventh, one of the two.

Looney said it was a small world.

"Hear you're up," Tompkins said to Trotter. "Buy me a beer. I had a day like that, once, it was in '56 at Santa Anita. I arrive at the track with twenty-two fifty and hit five in a row and am up fourteen grand and that was when fourteen grand was worth thirteen grand, the good old days."

Marty said the only thing good about the good old

days was everybody was younger, that's all. He gave Tompkins a beer on Trotter. The way Trotter was buying, he was sure *ACTING* like a winner.

"Streak-wise, I was hot," Tompkins continued. "Momentum-wise, I had it. I pick out a beauty in the sixth and bet everything but a dime. Guess what happened?"

"You won?"

"Are you crazy? Ass-wise, I lost. All but a dime. Still, it was one of the greatest days in my life."

Trotter requested a deck of cards from Marty.

It's a shame there isn't something they can hook to your arms and test you for luck. Hook electrodes to your skull or something and read you some horses and record your brain waves. You can check if a guy is lying. There is one fairly reliable exam you can take, but it isn't foolproof. It's called stud poker. You shuffle the cards and deal one down and four up and whoever has the best hand wins, unless you choke and fold a winner.

Trotter shuffled and Reardon cut.

Trotter dealt Looney one down and himself one down, and then he dealt one up to each player.

After four cards, Looney had a pair of kings showing, which is very good.

"If this was for money, I would bet a lot," Looney smiled to his pal.

"Call and raise sixty thousand," Trotter said.

He had three hearts up.

Looney said, "Well, I mean, it's all for fun. So. Call. Is that okay?"

Looney drew a third king. "Wow," he said.

Trotter's last card was the ace of hearts, which completed an ace, king, queen, jack, nine heart flush. That is one heart-beat from a royal flush. When Trotter turned his hole card over and exposed his hand, the room became silent.

Marty coughed. "That's very impressive. Good hand."

Trotter took the remainder of the deck from Reardon and spread the cards face down on the table. Trotter removed a card from the pack. He said, "I have a feeling this card is the five of clubs."

Nobody said a word.

Trotter held the card in his hand. "Want to see?"

"Listen, how about a round on the house," Marty said.

Sid Booten reached over and took the card and jammed it back in the deck. Nobody would ever know.

"I know," Trotter said.

That was a little scary.

THERE WAS AN HOUR BEFORE THE FEATURE, THE ninth race.

A call came on the pay phone for Trotter.

He grabbed the dangling receiver Marty left and took a deep breath and said, "Damn it, don't get mad, I won a fortune."

The answer was, "Who's mad?"

It was not his wife. It was a fellow named Claude Herron, who identified himself as a reporter for *Racing Times*, which was this magazine.

"So?" Trotter said.

"So it's one big hustle. There are about forty racing magazines and the way you sell copies is you get the big stories, the human interest jobs."

"So?"

"You're human. You're interesting. You're winning. It's the third qualification that catches the eye."

191

Claude Herron explained, quickly, that this track was his beat, and that the officials had suggested Trotter as an interesting subject. He was across the street in the press box. Why didn't he run across for a quick interview?

Claude brought a camera and took a group picture of Trotter and his friends in front of the painting of Citation. Claude Herron had to ask Trotter's friends to smile about a dozen times.

Reardon stood next to Trotter, scowling, one hand on his holster, in case this Claude Herron was a punk.

Trotter explained how he had accumulated a metal box full of money, exactly the way it happened, except for the mini-fraud there at the start—the part with the tape, and the encounter with Adams, the trainer. Claude Herron listened and wrote. Cent signs spun in his head. A feature story like this was worth a bonus. Claude Herron was a wrinkled up little fellow who smoked cigars that smelled like dried cow chips. A cow chip comes out of a cow. The odor was so bad, you could *notice* it, even in here.

Trotter's story, revealed for the first time to those regulars in attendance, almost qualified Trotter to be one of the boys again. It was such blind luck! But not quite. You just don't go around winning a bundle without paying the price. A few more rounds on the house, and THEN maybe Trotter could stick around, just like the old days.

Trotter's survey about knocked Claude Herron out of his chair.

He kept saying, "Really? Come on. Really? You're kidding. Really? You took a survey and then went and did the *OPPOSITE*?"

"People are usually wrong," Trotter said. "You can quote me. The average guy is usually nuts."

"You *REALLY* did that survey?"

Trotter showed Claude Herron the notes he had kept.

Claude Herron ran outside into the light and took a picture of Trotter holding the remnants of his survey.

When the reporter had all the facts, he asked Trotter what he was going to do with the money, let it ride or what? Invest in land? Take a cruise? Pork bellies? What?

"I don't know."

Claude Herron said every story has to have an ending.

"What would *YOU* do?" Trotter asked him.

"Me? Hell, I'd be farther away from this place than here."

"Not me." Looney said. "I'd bet the whole thing, every penny. All or nothing."

Herron asked if he could hang with Trotter until the story ended.

"If you stay downwind with that cigar."

CLAUDE HERRON THOUGHT HE HAD TWO TREMENdous human interest feature stories for *Racing Times*.

Lufkin about went for a guy named Tompkins' throat. It looked like good copy.

That was until Johnny Casino said nobody does no writing around here except me.

He held the door open for Lufkin, who came in like a firefighter, with a handkerchief over his mouth, waving at the smoke with his free hand.

Many guys tried to blend into the woodwork, but couldn't find it in all the smoke.

"This place ought to be condemned," Lufkin said. "Somebody open a window."

"What's a window?" Looney asked.

Lufkin congratulated Trotter on his display of

skill, said he couldn't believe it, said he'd never heard it done, but be that as it may, where the exact hell was Tompkins?

Johnny Casino called Tompkins like a naughty dog. "Here, Tompkins." Nobody said that Tompkins was here a second ago.

"In fifteen minutes, Tompkins will be five minutes late with some money," Lufkin said. "Three to two he's in the john."

He was.

He showed himself, and sat down.

"Tompkins," Lufkin said, "how's things in the john?"

"Just fine."

"That's good. What's his number, Johnny?"

"Two-twenty."

"Pay me, Tompkins."

Tompkins began shaking money out of his shoes, pockets and hat. He scooped bills and change into a pile on the table and began counting it.

"Tompkins, you need a new hobby, you know?" Lufkin said. "Now, I don't say this to everybody, do I, Johnny? I just go about my business of providing a service and let the chips fall where they may."

"Money-wise," Tompkins said, "it's going to be close." He had counted to one-eighty, and things were getting slim, there in the pile.

"Tompkins, I tell you this like, well, like maybe a cousin-in-law. The point is, not like a stranger. You got to quit betting. I been at this a long time, Tompkins, what, Johnny, thirty-five years? I been at it since they were hacking guys apart and throwing them in the river. A guy was two seconds late back then, they'd crack his head, no questions. Now listen, Tompkins. You're the worst I ever saw."

When it became possible Tompkins would run

out of cash before he got to two-twenty, he started counting slower.

"I got this brother," Tompkins said.

"Really, Tompkins. I swear to Christ. You're the worst I ever saw, heard of, or could imagine. You got to stop this. It breaks my heart."

"And this brother of mine is a lawyer," Tompkins said, counting real slow.

"Listen to this," Lufkin said to the boys. "Tompkins has got it bad. Tompkins, the only reason I would make a man's bet public is to run him off, for your own good, you know. Boys, Tompkins once made a bet on the CIRCUS. I mean it. Nothing is going on, between seasons and all, so Tompkins calls and has me make a line on the lion tamer, and get ready for this, fucking Tompkins bets on the lions to eat the guy! Can you believe that?"

"My brother is a great lawyer," Tompkins said. "Right out of the Ivy League."

"And listen to this," Lufkin continued. "Once Tompkins bet this high school game, I make him a special number, and the other team gets pissed off and leaves the field! Some bad call. Okay, the other team leaves the field! Now the team Tompkins bet on, they run a play against fucking nobody, right? Nobody is out there. You know what play they run? A pass! I mean for the love of God, nobody out there, so you sneak it. This kid goes back and throws one, and it falls incomplete! Against nobody! There's not even any damn wind! Tompkins' team can't score against nobody. Tompkins, you got to find another outlet, I mean it."

"My brother the lawyer says it would be interesting if some guy like me who owed a bookie like you took it to court. He says since gambling with a bookie is illegal, the court might rule in my favor and I don't gotta pay. My brother says there's no law that says you have to pay for something illegal."

Lufkin said, "Tompkins, you're about to be in trouble. There's the law of the jungle, Tompkins. Are you saying you're not going to settle up? Are you saying you're going to take me to court? Oh, Tompkins. Tell me it's all the smoke in the air that made me hear you wrong. Please tell me that."

Tompkins had $223. He scooted the $220 to Lufkin, who scooted it to Johnny.

"I was just kidding," Tompkins said. "About the other."

"I'll tell you one thing," Reardon said to Johnny Casino. "If I was on duty, I'd put the cuffs on you for general principles. I don't like a thing about you. In fact, the *BEST* thing I like about you is those no-good shoes."

Marty interrupted the various conversations before somebody hastily pulled a gun and started shooting holes in Citation.

"Do you want the safe open or not?" he asked Trotter.

It was behind Citation, over the bar.

"Tell you what, Marty," Trotter said. Everybody watched Trotter with great interest. It was like he was going to say something worthy of a history book; Claude Herron *DID* have his pen out. "I'll just keep the money with me awhile. No big deal. I've got my own personal safe already paid for."

Trotter nodded at Reardon.

Reardon dramatically placed his left hand on the money box.

"You're the boss," Reardon said.

Nobody else said a thing for perhaps thirty seconds. Then Looney said, "Well, goddamn it, come on!"

Looney reminded Trotter of Lawrence of Arabia,

giving the order to swoop down on a train. Looney was magnificent as he rose from his chair through the smoke and let out a tremendous war whoop, one of such velocity, it woke a couple of drunks up.

"Who died?" one asked.

At Looney's urging, Trotter received a rousing cheer from the others. Even Vibes Eberhart was impressed. He momentarily cast aside his personal trauma and applauded.

"Now that's a man," Evangeline said to Sid Booten, rising from her chair.

"It's easy to be a man when you have money," Sid said.

"Guess-wise, the guy's gonna shoot all of it," Tompkins said to Lufkin.

"First, the guy embarrasses me by ordering a martini," Marty said to Johnny Casino. "Then he orders dinner from a Chinese joint and has it *delivered*. Now, he doesn't like my safe. Nobody's stole a grilled cheese in twenty years from that safe. The next thing you know, he'll open a lemonade stand on the curb. Still, you have to admire somebody with that much intestinal fortitude."

"He'll be back," Johnny said. "I seen all kinds, shapes, and sizes. He'll be back to me. I'll be knocking on his door, collecting. An hour from now, he'll kill for a twenty. They're all alike. They're all losers."

Still, Johnny had to whistle during Trotter's cheer. The guy *did* have guts, balls, and heart, the three most important things in the world. Brains is fourth.

It was like Trotter gave birth, which he did in a way; he gave birth to a new concept in investing: shooting it all on a horse. At least that's what everybody thought Trotter would do as they stopped by the table to offer congratulations on the decision.

"All I said is I have a guy to guard the money, so

why pay Marty twenty bucks safe rental?" Trotter said a couple of times feebly.

"It's funny," Marty said to Lufkin. "Here my pick of the day in the first race comes in second. Loses a photo. Nobody even knows I'm alive."

"Bet some football and I'll know you're alive," Lufkin said.

Reardon had everybody line up and wish Trotter the best, one at a time. No gangs, he said. No swarms. He had relaxed his rule about no punks. They were everywhere. "You really need to develop a new circle of friends," Reardon whispered. "I've never seen so many weirdos in my life, and I've worked some pretty grim neighborhoods, believe you me."

"Future-wise, good luck, pal," Tompkins said.

It was like Trotter was a hit man.

Trotter again said, "All I said was...ah, the hell with it."

Those regulars in Marty's concluded that you HAD to like a guy like that. Now, if he bet HALF the cash, that was another matter. You don't have to like a guy like *that*. That's forsaking friendship for personal gain. But when a guy risks it all, listen, that's class. You let everything ride, the downside risk is like jumping off Pikes Peak.

They'd by God drink to that, to letting it ride.

So Trotter bought a round for his pals.

If he lost, they'd by God be there when it was over, when he needed THEM; they'd drink to what might have been.

If somebody would only buy.

So set 'em up!

They sure hoped he'd bet it all.

Trotter could have taken Wild Turkey in the vein and stayed sober. He had had approximately ten beers, six Wild Turkeys, two martinis, and the banana thing in the Jockey Club that smelled like Old Spice. He was nevertheless in complete control of his senses as he walked to the pay phone to call Pam.

You remember her. So did Trotter.

She was, strangely enough, home.

She answered on the first ring.

"Hi, honey," Trotter said.

"Don't honey me," Pam said. "Besides, I'm drunk."

"You know the race? The one you left before? You know that one?"

"I've decided to be an alcoholic. There's really nothing to it, except it makes my stomach hurt."

"I won. That race. We're pretty rich."

"I'm going to drink every day, morning, noon, and night. I'm going to hide bottles around the house. I'm never going to cook, clean, or take baths. I'm going to quit shaving. It's the only way. So you see, I don't care. You can sell the bed to make bets with. I'll just be passing out on the floor from here on in. Better yet, sell the damn icebox and the stove. Sell the sink."

"I've got the money here in a box."

"Oh, how nice, but then, I'm drunk and that's why that's nice and that's that. Why don't you bet what you won on a car race or something? That would be nice. Nice, nice, nice."

"I haven't bet any of it, Pam."

"Oh, you'll bet it. But I don't care, you see, because I'm drunk. You can bet it all. Really. I know you will. You can't fool me. I'm flicking ashes on the floor. It's really fun. I'm drinking gin and flicking ashes on the floor and the TV is flicking and I don't give a... damn, is what. I don't give a hoot. What it came down to was becoming drunk or going mad, so I chose drunk. So you go make your little bet and call when you get around to it. I'll be here. I may be passed out in a pool of vomit, but I'll be here. Okay?"

"Damn it, I did it for us," Trotter said.

"That's so sweet."

Tompkins slapped Trotter on the back.

"Anything else we need from the market?"

"Some wine," Pam said. "And beer. And mix. How is your big-tittied friend, Miss whatever her name was? She had such a nice personality. You ought to have her over sometime."

"Listen, I love you," Trotter whispered.

"Thank you. That's very kind. Good luck."

"You mean it?"

"Yes, of course I mean it. Who is this?"

Trotter said he would not be late.

"Late, early, what's the difference."

"I'll be sure and pick up the bread," Trotter said, and he put the phone back.

He waved at Reardon and got into the money box to pay Marty for the rounds, plus there was a nice tip. "Okay," Trotter said. "Let's go."

Reardon said, "You got it."

The procession swept out the front door, about emptying the joint.

"You're really great for business," Marty shouted to Trotter.

Claude Herron did his best to record accurately this electric moment, *whatever* it meant. He interviewed several members of the party.

Vibes Eberhart tried to explain his system to Herron, about conjuring up visions on *ANY* sport, but the reporter cut him short with questions about Trotter. "The guy will blow it all. It's classic. Self-destructive, the whole bit. Now about my system . . ."

Looney said that Trotter, and this was for print, was, "One of the great people of our day. A real friend. A trooper."

"But has he ever picked horses this good before?"

"Are you kidding?"

Looney almost let something slip out about the blood bank, but decided it wouldn't look good in black and white, so he clammed up.

Sid Booten said he had known Trotter maybe a year. "He's pretty heavy. I, Sid Booten, would have personally wheeled the horse in the first and doubled up in the second to get back the juice from the basket I lost last night. Playing the hoops and the grids and the ponies at the same time is a real test of courage, is hard to get into and down on."

"You what?" Claude Herron asked.

Evangeline said she only had a second to give the reporter. She was busy tracing bloodlines in the *Form*. "Trotter is kind of cute."

TROTTER STOPPED AT THE CURB ACROSS FROM THE track, thought a moment, and said to Reardon, "This way." He went right, past a nice motel that jacked its rates up triple during the meet, and a sleazy dump behind that advertised, "All You Can Sleep, $9.95." You could keep a horse in the room for fity cents extra.

Trotter walked a block and a half and went into George's, which was a very exclusive men's clothing store. George had Dobermans by his desk. Real ones. This neighborhood was a little rough around the edges, so a man couldn't be too careful. The reason there is an exclusive place near the track is the reason you see stores selling mink coats in the fancy casinos in Las Vegas. You're not talking volume, you're talking a few really big scores from winners. You sell one mink a week, that's fine. A guy gets hot at the track, his first inclination is to spend a little something, step out, move up in class. George was not born yesterday.

George took one look at the pack that followed Trotter inside and mopped his brow.

"Attention," he said to his dogs.

"Sit the goddamn dogs down," Reardon said, fingering his holster. "Unless you want them pushing up dogwoods."

"That's pretty funny," Trotter said to Reardon. "Pushing up dogwoods."

"Oh my," George said. "Sit." The presence of a uniformed cop was calming. The presence of the money box also helped.

As George smiled at the money box, Reardon said, "That's enough of that."

Looney was looking at a rack. "People REALLY buy this stuff?"

Johnny Casino was looking at some green shoes made of the stuff you play miniature golf on, the stuff you cover patios with, THAT kind of stuff. "How much?"

"Eighty," George said.

"Eighty *WHAT*?" Looney asked. "Box tops?"

Outside, Claude Herron was visiting with a couple of new members of the bandwagon, Solly Friedman the un-Jewish tip sheet wizard, and Mickey Jax, the tipster who had a winner every race: himself.

Solly Friedman gave Claude Herron a free copy of the *Kosher Nag* and said it might be nice to mention in whatever story he was doing that he, Solly Friedman, was starting a new telephone service where he picked football winners, with a money-back guarantee. The way the phone tip service worked was Solly Friedman took a pro game, say the Giants and Jets. Say the betting number was the Giants, favored by seven. You call Solly for his pick. To one guy, he says, "Giants." To the next guy he says, "Jets." He alternates the picks. You, the customer, don't pay unless

Solly gives you the winner. Obviously, by picking one team one call, the other team next call, Solly is right on half the calls. Say he gets one hundred calls on the Giants-Jets. He gives fifty people the winner. The guys who lose don't pay. The ones who win send in $25. That's $1,250 a night, not caring *WHO* wins.

Solly was on top of it, all right.

Of course, he didn't tell Claude Herron that he, Solly Friedman, was a conniving, ornery, there's-one-born-every-minute hustler. What he said was he had a tip phone service that was the best in the business. You don't win, you don't pay. What could be fairer?

Claude Herron asked for and received the number to call.

"There's *TWO* born every minute," Mickey Jax whispered to Solly Friedman. "You crooks."

"There's the pot calling the kettle a crock," Solly winked.

Trotter?

Yeah, they knew him.

A loser on recess.

Trotter bought a patchwork sports coat for three hundred dollars, the hell with the tax, okay, George?

Okay.

Trotter took his windbreaker off and pitched it in a trash can and slipped his coat over his knit shirt.

One of the dogs barked.

"He likes it," George said. "He only barks when he likes it. It looks great with jeans, too."

Johnny Casino bought the green shoes, and wore them out.

"You know what you look like?" Looney asked. Looney was standing next to Reardon. "Like a frog."

"Back off," Reardon said. "He's right."

"When the jacket wears out," Tompkins said,

"you can always use it as a quilt, Trotter. Money-wise, it was a good investment."

"You like the shoes?" Johnny Casino asked Lufkin.

Trotter stopped in a store next door and bought a $750 necklace and sent it to his wife.

"Where to," Reardon asked. "Now?"

Trotter looked up at the track. "Back there."

"You damn right," Reardon said.

"We can do it," Looney said.

"Classic case," Vibes Eberhart said.

"You like the shoes?" Johnny Casino asked Lufkin.

"You look like an elf."

"This is exciting, sweetheart," Sid Booten said to Evangeline.

"What's mudder mean?" she asked anybody.

"It means the horse is so old, it's got sons and daughters," Mickey Jax said. "You're not bad, honey, if you'd get that wire out of your mouth. You want a winner this race?"

"Leave her alone," Sid Booten said.

"Why don't you both dry up and let a person concentrate," Evangeline said.

A cop stopped traffic so that the procession could safely cross the street. "That jacket he bought could have stopped traffic," Vibes Eberhart said.

Trotter asked Reardon for a twenty for Shiela's pot. She was shaking her bell almost as much as she was shaking her butt.

"Hey, Trotter, thanks. That'll feed one starving kid. Me."

Once inside the main gate, Reardon asked again, "Where to?"

"The bathroom."

"Damn right."

Rudy was in the process of being arrested for operating a cigar box without a license. Trotter told the guards there was a rape and a mugging over by the beer stand, and the guards left, and Rudy slipped off, with his sincere thanks and the cigar box.

Reardon stood guard.

Trotter removed his jacket and washed his hands and dried his face with a free towel, the way God intended.

"Where to?"

"Outside. The rail."

"Damn right."

BERNIE GREENBERG THOUGHT IT WAS A FIGHT AND didn't pay much attention. He was in no mood to pay anything else, anyway, the way he had been losing.

He merely glanced at the activity below, by the finish line, and went back to the *Racing Form*. It looked like a maze.

Joy (Miss Backstretch), however, took a long look at the pushing and shoving beneath her. She didn't have anything else to do. The small sum she had won had been plucked back by Bernie, who had turned jerk. She had been severely chastised for flirting, looking like a go-go dancer, and playing footsie.

"I guess there's some perverse pleasure you get going around half-naked," Bernie said.

"Can I have a dollar, Bernie?"

"No." He got mean when he lost.

"It was an accident, the blouse popped, Bernie,"

She got up and went to the ladies' room.

The blouse was fastened with a safety pin. Barely.

"Come back," Harvey the waiter said. "Please, I beg you."

SIMPSON, THE MOVER OF MEN, WAS BESIDE HIMSELF.

He thought it was a joke at first, but then recovered quickly and stepped back to consider the matter at hand. It was going to be very tricky, clearing fifteen spaces at the rail for Mr. Trotter's party.

He gave Trotter a group rate at four dollars a head.

Trotter said forget it, and had Reardon give Simpson a fresh C-note.

"I think it's a two-owner bill," Trotter said. "Some poor slob and the track."

"Don't worry about a thing," Simpson nodded. "Just relax, Trotter. I guarantee, it's in the bag."

Simpson announced to those regulars and tourists to the left of the finish line, "Let's get all the women off the rail for about twenty-five yards."

"Why?" some character with binoculars asked. This was a touchy time for space-clearing, as the eighth, the race before the feature, was five minutes from starting.

"Because I say so," Simpson said. "That's why. I'm going to clear fifteen spaces right HERE, so unless you want that woman there squashed like a sardine, you better get her back."

"You can't do that."

"Is that a statement or is that famous last words?"

The guy and his wife stepped back.

"I'm not sure this is legal," Reardon said.

"Look the other way," Trotter told him.

A substantial crowd had gathered by the finish line at the rail, and Simpson's antics were not very popular, particularly with those people who had been staking out a good spot for hours before the feature.

"Hey, what's going on up there?"

"Hey, you big lug, get the hell out of the way."

"Stop pushing."

"Knock it off."

Simpson placed his huge mitts on the shoulders of one of his assistants, and he began wading left, slowly at first, like an ox. Simpson was leaning forward and grunting.

Somebody up the way lost his footing and that was all the leverage Simpson needed. He had momentum and cleared the proper number of spaces in thirty seconds flat.

There were a few shouts and threats until Simpson straightened up and asked, "Who said that?"

Nobody had said that.

What somebody had said was, "They're off."

THE EIGHTH RACE WAS NOTHING TO WIRE HOME about, unless you needed bus fare.

A gray won, sending goose bumps up and down the limbs of countless Jewish ladies who bet two dollars to show.

"I can't believe it," Solly Friedman said. "I *HAD* it. I *HAD* the gray to win."

Claude Herron asked Trotter please to describe what was going on in his head at this very moment, as he stood at the finish line with many thousands of dollars in cash, as he stood precariously on the threshold of, perhaps, immortality.

"Nothing," Trotter said.

Herron did not write this down.

Joy (Miss Backstretch) had no trouble at all working her way to the rail. The reason was, everybody stepped back for a look. She slipped in behind Trotter and put her arms around his stomach and said, "Guess who, sweetie?"

Trotter had known who was there before Miss Backstretch had spoken. He had known even before she placed her breasts on his back. He had known she was in the area when a man somewhere behind them said, "My God, look what happened to that blouse! Look what's under what's left of that blouse!"

To "Guess who, sweetie?" Trotter said, "A football salesman."

"Don't be naughty," Miss Backstretch said.

"I'm happily married, I think," Trotter said.

Miss Backstretch wondered what that had to do with anything and Trotter said he didn't know, so she kissed him on the cheek.

"A kiss is just a kiss."

"How's your friend up there in the penthouse?"

"Bernie can be a creep, but he's got a lot of money, which comes in handy sometimes. Plus, he can't make love for ten days after he has a bad losing streak."

"No kidding," Trotter said.

"No. A girl has to decide what's important, money or love. Both together are real nice. This is the twentieth century, you know. I was thinking, you're real emotional. Bernie has the insides of an adding machine. I just saw you out here and came down. That's all. I'm getting a little nervous now. I was thinking about asking you to go to bed because you're kind of funny, that's all."

"Oh."

Claude Herron asked Miss Backstretch if she was an old friend of Trotter's.

"No, I'm twenty-one," she answered.

He did not write that down, either.

Miss Backstretch slinked next to Trotter at the rail.

Simpson cleared the space, on the house, he said, for the pleasure of being in the company of such a lovely young lady.

Reardon was to Trotter's right, being peripheral.

"You try to arrest her for indecent exposure, I'll fire you," Trotter said.

"She's decent," Reardon said. "She's BETTER than decent."

When Miss Backstretch leaned over the rail to look for the horses, so did everybody else.

THE GOOD THING ABOUT A FEATURE RACE AT A GOOD track is the quality rises to the bait, the bait being cash.

The bad thing is, it is as hard to pick a winner from a field of good horses as it is to pick a winner from a field of scarecrows.

The good ones just get around the track faster, that's all.

It was assumed by all that Trotter would bet the feature. He looked at the smiling faces around him. If I don't bet, they'll lynch me, he thought.

Word that Trotter had removed the *Racing Form* from the back pocket of his jeans was quickly passed up and down the rail. This was followed by word that he had unfolded it, and then the message was passed, he's opening the *Form* to the feature!

Everybody was depressed when Trotter rolled the *Form* into a tight little bat and bashed a horsefly on the rail.

Claude Herron leaned over the rail and sketched Miss Backstretch's profiles in case the magazine

REALLY wanted to sell a few copies next month.

Trotter glanced at the feature in the *Racing Form* —it was his duty—but it looked like a dog's breakfast. All the entries had potential. Tompkins had bought a little biorhythm guidebook and was down in the stables trying to find the exact hour when each horse was born.

Trotter decided that finding a secret sign in all the numbers was similar to trying to identify twins, from the back, so he pitched the *Racing Form* over the rail, into the drainage ditch. A couple of others did likewise.

"What do you think?" Trotter asked Looney.

"We may never go this way again," Looney said.

"What does THAT mean?"

"It means, I don't know, it means this might be a chance of a lifetime."

"So was the race I just won," Trotter said.

"Good point," Looney agreed.

"What do YOU think?" Trotter asked Vibes Eberhart.

"I think you ought to donate your brain to science. The fact you're HERE, the fact you're even inside this place, AT THE RAIL, that proves to me you're not playing with a full deck."

Reardon was not paid to think.

"What do you think?" Trotter asked Miss Backstretch.

"Go for it," she said. "But what are you talking about?"

"Look at this," Looney said. He had the program, where the entries and jockeys and the Morning Lines were listed. Looney was tapping his finger at the four horse.

"So?" Trotter said.

"It's won four in a row."

Trotter was more taken with the two horse.

Its name was Hot to Trot, the last part of which was the first part of Trotter's very own name. The "Hot" part also had a nice ring to it.

TIME FLIES WHEN YOU'RE HAVING FUN. IT ALSO FLIES when you're not having fun.

Sometimes time flies first class, like in the Jockey Club.

The damn stuff *always* flies, though.

The pressure was getting to Trotter, there was no doubt about it. There was no TIME to make a mature decision about anything.

It was about five minutes before the horses would be paraded by the grandstand.

"Listen," Trotter said so everybody could hear. "Here's the deal. I've got a horse picked out."

They knew it.

"What we'll do now is take everything we have, every penny, and we'll all put it in a pile, and go bet it. We'll all be in it together."

Sid Booten frowned so hard, he could barely see out.

"I'm with you," Looney said. "Only I don't have any money."

Nobody else said anything.

It was all too clear; Trotter was incoherent.

THEY CAME ONTO THE TRACK LIKE BATHING BEAUTIES, prancing slightly, then they took a left and went by the grandstand, slowly, the way the latest in nuclear weaponry is paraded by heads of governments.

"I give the swimsuit competition to the four

horse," Looney said. "Star Gazer. That is one good-looking animal."

Mickey Jax had passed out his tips as freely as campaign buttons, tipping THREE ladies on the four horse, Star Gazer, because he liked it. Tipping three ladies on one horse was like betting the horse yourself, so Mickey had a vested interest in the feature, and planned even to cheer, if he remembered how. Sometimes, tipping three ladies on the same horse got a little wicked because each lady thought Mickey loved her and her alone. If all three of them showed up to pay Mickey off with a kiss and some cash, there might be a little scratching. Tipping three ladies on the same horse isn't REALLY like betting, because you can't *lose* with a tip, but it's nice to have something to yell for. Mickey hadn't yelled for a horse in so long, it was hard on his lungs, which felt like they were full of little chug holes that had been patched up with tar. He cleared his throat and said, "Come on four," and then he wheezed.

Solly Friedman had wandered off to accept congratulations from a gang of Jewish women for hitting the last gray. He was laying it on thick, about how intensely he studied the horses before making a selection for his tip sheet.

Lufkin was hanging around in case Trotter WAS hot and wanted to keep betting things like football into the wee hours.

His caddy, Johnny Casino, he left.

What happened was, his new green shoes went up like straw.

Somebody accidentally, perhaps, flipped a cigarette ash on Johnny's right shoe and within seconds the left shoe was also flaming. He looked like a circus clown, running for the exit.

"Those shoes could revolutionize the charcoal-

212

broiling industry," Looney said to Trotter.

Reardon said nothing about starting a fire without a permit in a congested area, so he must have done it.

Evangeline had decided to bet all two hundred of her dollars on the four horse, Star Gazer, to show.

"But, honey," Sid Booten said. "It's hard to win a lot of money that way."

"Sid, you're getting on my nerves. I think what we need to concentrate on is not *losing* money."

Lufkin put his hand on Evangeline's hip and asked if she could take dictation. Evangeline said she could take it just fine, but getting it down on paper was another matter.

"Get that fence out of your mouth, you got a chance, kid," Lufkin said.

"Listen you. You're old enough to be my dermatologist. Tell him, Sid."

"She still goes to one. She's only nineteen. It's the braces that make her look older. She's got to frown a lot to keep her lips closed."

Lufkin passed down the line on the lone night football game, the Rams at the Forty-Niners. The Rams were a ten-point favorite. Trotter looked at the slip of paper and put it in the pocket of his new jacket.

Vibes Eberhart had his hands on the rail, his head down, and he was breathing deeply. A woman tourist from Topeka told her husband that somebody should get a stomach pump, that guy was ill.

"He is communicating with the dead," Looney informed the tourist. "He is trying to reach that Great Handicapper in the Sky, that's all."

"Four," Vibes moaned. "FOUR!"

"Oh crap, hurry up and putt out, Trotter," Looney said. "Vibes is playing through."

"Four!"

"Here's a four-iron," Looney said, handing Vibes a rolled-up program. "Knock it on the green, pardner. You can do it."

Looney again scrutinized the four horse. "Is truly a beautiful animal."

"So are polar bears," Trotter said, "But they can't run. This is no zoo."

Claude Herron reminded Trotter it was fifteen minutes until post time. "The two-dollar windows really get crowded before the feature." Herron then realized that the only possible business Trotter would have at the two-dollar window would be buying it and taking it home to convert into a nice little wet bar. "Sorry," Claude said. "It's just, I'm getting a little nervous myself."

Trotter looked at the horses when they walked past him up the track. The race was a mile. They would start right here.

It was amazing how little their legs were, how fragile.

It would be like putting glass roller skates on the Buick.

It could have been an optical illusion, but Trotter thought the two horse, Hot to Trot, looked right into his eyes before the jockey, a mini-man named White, jogged the horse up the track.

"You see that?" Trotter asked Reardon.

"I saw a guy twenty yards right take a lighter out of another guy's coat," Reardon said.

"Horses are so pretty," Miss Backstretch said.

That was relative, Trotter guessed. He had bet on a destruction derby once, and won something like $7.50, and thought the car that won was beautiful, all right. Line some cows up and paint some numbers on their butts and put a hundred on one of them, she'd probably look pretty.

It's all in the eye of the beholder.

Trotter doubted that ten thousand people would stand behind a fence and say, "Oh, what beautiful animals," if they weren't about to race their guts out.

Besides, beauty is only fin deep.

Trotter requested that Reardon remove one crisp fin from the money box. Reardon did so with great care. Trotter put the five-dollar bill in his pocket and said to Looney, "I've decided to bet the race."

Looney smiled understandingly. "It's the only way. Don't worry, I'll still be here. I'm *WITH* you. So are your friends."

"You don't understand, Looney. I'm going to WIN the race."

"You are?"

"That's right."

"You damn right!" Reardon said. "We are!"

"There's a big tip in this for you, Reardon."

"Thank you," he said. "We can by God do it!"

"Jesus," Miss Backstretch said, gasping. "I'm so excited. All over. Everywhere there is. This is what life is all about. Spontaneity, if you know what I mean."

"I do," Trotter said. He kissed her on the cheek to prove it.

"Bernie, he has got to have a Dean Martin record on, and everything just so. He schedules it, like a business meeting! That's yucky."

Trotter motioned for Simpson and requested that his space at the rail be secured.

"I'm going to bet."

Simpson rubbed Trotter's head like he was a little kid.

"You can't save space out here," somebody said. "This is first come, first serve."

Simpson said the only kind of service he was familiar with was where you knocked something or somebody over a net.

Reardon cleared a path through the crowd you could have driven a Brink's truck through.

"I MAY FAINT," MURDOCK, THE TICKET SELLER SAID.

Trotter said nothing.

"Look, honey," a woman from Boston said. "That guy over there is betting a box! I thought you had to bet money. It must be an antique box or something."

"Must," her husband said.

Reardon had placed the money box on the counter. Trotter said he was going to let it ride.

"It's okay," Murdock said. "We have major medical. If I faint, I'm covered. Is it all in there? *All* of it?"

"Basically," Trotter answered. "I bought some things."

"Nice coat."

"And I kept out five dollars. But it's generally all there."

"All those thousands, right?"

"Sixty-eight or so."

"There are all kinds of balls," Murdock said. "I hope one of yours is a crystal."

Murdock pushed a button under the counter. "Needless to say, I can't push you fifty-dollar win tickets."

"Needless."

"It would take all week. That would be, what, one thousand, three hundred and sixty win tickets. We haven't GOT that many. You'd have to carry them on a donkey. The machine would short out, you know?"

Men in suits arrived at Murdock's window and the situation was explained, and one of them said,

"This way," opening a swinging gate that led behind the windows.

Trotter and Reardon were led through a room where money was being stacked, pounds of money. One man was ironing crinkled cash. Reardon said he didn't think the track would lose any sleep, regardless of who won the feature. They were finally deposited in a small room where what appeared to be an Arab sheik was trying to do business with a man who sat at a desk behind the name plate of Pink.

Mr. Pink was saying, "Now, my good man, please talk slowly so we won't make an error. Take your time."

"What is it I want to say to get across message of superior importance that has to do with upcoming wager."

The Arab said this to what Trotter and Reardon assumed was an interpreter. This interpreter nodded, and said to Mr. Pink, "What want to say about race to make bet?"

"I think the guy is trying to make a bet," Reardon said to Trotter, who thought so too.

"Want to say considerable importance about race that is feature," the head Arab said. He wore a flowing garb that touched the floor.

"Yes, yes," the interpreter said. "Feature of race."

"You want a bet on the feature?" Mr. Pink asked.

"Is that," the interpreter said.

"You give me a horse and the amount you wish to wager," Mr. Pink said, wiping his brow, "and I'll give you a receipt, similar to what you would have received at a regular window. Okay?"

"Yes, good. Have many of horses. How many of horses you want? Have beautiful. Gift of horses for wife, yes? Payola, yes?"

"No, no," Mr. Pink said. "God, no. What I mean is

217

you give a horse's number and what you want to bet in the feature and I'll take the bet for you."

"Means what, number of horse of the feature?" the head Arab asked the interpreter. They huddled. Mr. Pink looked at Trotter and Reardon and sighed.

"That is good," the head Arab said. "I give you number. You give me money."

"Yes, yes," Mr. Pink said. "If you win, you come back here with the receipt and I give you money."

"Good, good."

"What number do you want? What horse?"

"I want horse the six. Is the o'clock I make first million. Six o'clock, June 6. All sixes. The oil, she comes up through cousin's pool of swimming. Is very beautiful thing to see, the oil, she come up very fast in country of my. Horse the six."

"Six," the interpreter said.

"Good, yes, I understand," Mr. Pink said. "How much?"

"Ah, that is question of much difficulty, how much. I think it would much beneficial to say wager of forty. Is age of my being, forty."

"Good. Forty what?"

"Dollars."

The Arab's interpreter plopped four tens on Mr. Pink's counter. Air escaped him, like he had been punctured. "Forty on six."

"Is correct and true," the Arab said.

He turned to Trotter and Reardon. "Is very bad place to spend time of day, out here. Pickers of pocket. Sometimes I carry snake in pocket of robe as lesson for people who have none of manners."

Mr. Pink gave the Arab the receipt, and the foreign guests were escorted out the door to their private box. "Sometimes he bets a hundred thousand, sometimes twenty dollars. You never know. The man is very unpredictable."

"*Sprechen zie German?*" Trotter said.

The color left Mr. Pink's cheeks.

Trotter said he was just kidding.

"Thank God. We get 'em all in here. What can I do for you?"

"I want every penny in that box on the two horse." Reardon put the box on Mr. Pink's desk. The money was bound in five-thousand bunches and therefore was easy to count.

Mr. Pink took the box and looked up at Trotter. "Don't worry, I'm not going to say anything, like, that's a lot of money. You've seen men come in here in rags and bet thousands, nothing surprises you. I make it sixty-seven, seven. That *IS* a lot of money."

Mr. Pink explained, since this was Trotter's first visit to the vault area, how this office worked. You were issued a receipt for the amount of the wager, and, of course, the horse, two, Hot to Trot. Now, what was nice about this particular operation was if you lost your receipt, you could still collect, unlike the regular tickets that have to be retained. The bet, of course, was immediately routed into the track's computer that adjusted odds on the tote board. Mr. Pink punched a button on a console computer on his desk and said the two horse was currently ten to one. He did some figuring and determined that a bet of this size would knock the odds down to approximately, 2, 2½–1.

When this happened, Trotter smiled to himself, when the news of his bet showed up on the tote board, everybody would say, "Boy, somebody knows something on the two horse."

Those who know better would probably say, "Well, some Arab's gone nuts again."

When Mr. Pink quickly filled out the proper information on the receipt and handed it to Trotter, Trotter said, "I'll see you back here in a few minutes."

"May I say one thing? You're certainly calm. It's very pleasant on this end. Some of the people who come in here are about to gnaw off a table leg."

"I'm going to win," Trotter said.

"I just work here," Mr. Pink said. "It's happened. I've seen people win. Excuse me."

Another Arab marched to the desk. "Is this place of superior wagering?"

Trotter and Reardon didn't use the private area under the press box reserved for people who bet ungodly boxes of money, so they were taken down an elevator to the ground floor. There was time for a beer, but only that.

Since Reardon had been paid, and since he didn't have anything left to guard judiciously, Trotter thanked him for his time and swell job, and told him he could take off if he wanted.

Reardon grabbed Trotter by the back of the neck. "Listen, pal. I've seen all kinds of punks. It goes with the territory. But let me tell you one thing. You've got the kind of pioneering spirit, the *spunk*, that makes a police officer proud to walk the streets. You don't take any crap from anybody. I'm with you, pal."

"Thanks, Reardon."

Trotter wondered why Reardon was offering yet another shoulder to weep on, instead of hanging around to guard the money and escort Trotter home when he won. Trotter mentioned that.

"We'll take that as it comes," Reardon said. "Tell me one thing. Why in the name of God did you bet *ALL* that money?"

"You don't think it was wise?"

"Boy, I don't know. I saw a TV show about a guy who bet a lot, everything he had. It ended with

220

him jumping off the Golden Gate Bridge."

"I'm going to win, Reardon. I really am. I'm on a hot streak. Things have been happening today that cannot be explained any other way. This horse is about the same as my name. What more could a person ask than a real shot at it?"

"Boy, I don't know."

"You want a beer, or you just want to stand there?" Quinella Hogan said. "Oh. Hi, Trotter."

"How about two on the house?" he said.

"To hell with you," Quinella said. "Times are tough. I'm ten short in the cash register, the way I've been losing."

"I'll buy," Reardon said.

"Put me in jail," Quinella said to Reardon. "So I can get a warm meal."

"You keep swearing and that's where you'll be."

Reardon explained to Quinella how it was possible for an off-duty cop to put the pinch on a citizen. "It takes about one second," Reardon said.

"Wait," Trotter said. "I've got five bucks. I kept it out. I forgot."

Rat-holing the five had been a reflex action. A voice from the past had told him to do it. You don't do things like that if you're on a hot roll. There's no *need*.

"Here, Quinella. Buy yourself a horse." Trotter gave her the five-dollar bill.

"Is this good?"

"Yeah."

"That's powerful," Reardon said to Trotter, giving him a beer.

"I haven't got a penny. Not one cent."

"Boy."

"I'm going to win."

"You really think so?"

"I *KNOW* so."

"There's one thing about that," Reardon said. "You haven't got any choice."

TROTTER THOUGHT, WALKING THROUGH THE CROWD back to the rail, "What if I lose?"

It was not a depressing exercise, though, because there was no consequence if he lost. He had eaten and consumed more than fifty dollars' worth, which was what he came to the track with, plus he had a new coat, and his wife had a new necklace, and he had made Looney and Jake the car park enormously happy by giving them money. He had also made new friends, like Miss Backstretch and Claude Herron the reporter and Murdock the ticket puncher and Reardon, and you cannot put a price tag on friendship, can you?

During this deep-think, Trotter bumped into Louie Kidder, tripped over him, actually. Louie is about four feet tall and he was checking the blacktop for money and tickets and combs, anything that had value. Trotter asked Louie what he would give for this beautiful sport coat.

Louie Kidder felt the material, "It's a little bright, but, um, it's good stuff. Since it's you, Trotter, thirty bucks and you don't even have to tell me where you stole it."

There was gas money home, and a nice dinner out somewhere.

But if he *won*, now there was something to think about.

So "What if I lose?" took about one minute to dismiss, and by the time Trotter got back to his spot at the rail, he had only touched the surface of "What if I win?" Trotter was smiling broadly and wondering what the poor people were doing at this very moment.

"Well?" Looney asked him. "I was worried. They're getting ready for the gate."

"Ah, I bet twenty bucks on the favorite."

Looney bit his lip and said, "Oh"

Sid Booten sniffed.

Lufkin said not to worry, it was a wise move, the easy stuff kicked off tonight, the stuff involving *humans*, not ignorant animals.

"Actually," Trotter said to Looney, "I bet every last penny on the two horse, the one that's similar to my name. How do you like that?"

"Goddamn," Looney shouted, "he did it! He shot it all, like we figured, on the two horse! When the number went down to 2–1 we figured you pissed it all away!"

"I've won, Looney."

They all crowded the rail to see what God thought of Trotter.

"It's out of our hands," Reardon said.

THE HORSES WENT INTO THE GATE.

They broke clean, on cue.

Trotter had planned to remain completely calm because a long stay in intensive care would quickly eat away the majority of his projected winnings. He planned to let nature take its course, may the best horse win, and raise his beer cup in a toast to honor a day that had been full of competition, good cheer, and brotherly love. A person does his best with what he has to work with. Here's to that, here's to living up to your potential. Trotter planned to say, beer cup at present arms, as his horse, two, embarked on his noble journey once neatly around the track.

You know what they say about spontaneity, though. It's emotional.

When the horses broke from the gate, Trotter excitedly threw his cup of beer on Looney, drenching him.

Looney grabbed his burning eyes, but not before he had said, "I think your two was limping coming out."

"Shut up or I'll kill you, you pessimistic jinx," Trotter said.

"I can't see," Looney said. "I'm going blind."

"Run, you son of a bitch!" Trotter yelled as his horse ran past.

"Oh, God," Miss Backstretch moaned, grabbing her breasts.

YOU COULD SEE NOTHING BUT REARS AS THEY WENT around the first turn, rears and tails and bobbing jockeys. Trotter had followed his jockey's colors, baby blue, out of the gate. His horse, two, was in the middle of the field. The jockey was high on the horse, which either meant things were well in hand or he was trying to get off.

Throughout the first turn is where the jockey rates the horse if the need arises. Rating a horse is where you keep it from putting out too much too soon.

Hot to Trot seemed to be on cruise-control.

Trotter started to pray to God, but there was no bad habit he could give up worth a pay-off of one hundred and eighty thousand dollars, with the possible exception of swearing to burn the new sport coat.

His horse went off at a strong 2–1, more like 2½.

He started a cigarette, took a swig of Bourbon from Simpson's bottle, and said, "Goddamn it."

He still felt empty, so he grabbed Miss Backstretch's left breast. Her hand was on it, so he grabbed her hand. It was the thought that counted.

He had smoked, drank, cussed, and grabbed at a breast in a span of ten seconds. He figured God hated fakers who made idle promises in pressure situations.

"If I win, I swear to God to give five dollars to Jerry Lewis, maybe," Trotter said.

Looney regained his vision and also heard what Trotter promised God if he won the race.

"I always swear to God to quit smoking," Looney said.

"The hell with it," Trotter yelled.

"I'd hate to be in your shoes," Looney sid.

"You ignorant bastard, this isn't a Billy Graham crusade. This is a horse race, by God."

Looney looked at the horses, fully expecting to see Trotter's number two fall to its knees in pain, then when that didn't happen, he looked at Trotter, expecting to see his eyes rolling.

"I bet you swore something to God secretly," Looney said.

"If I'm close coming for home, I can win the race," Trotter said.

"You better swear something to God quick."

"I swear to God if I'm close I'll win it, that's what I swear to God!"

"It just doesn't work that way," Looney mumbled.

"I swear to God if I *DON'T* win, I'll choke your chicken neck!"

"Easy," Reardon said, shaking Trotter by the shoulders. "You're right in the middle of it. Don't kill anybody yet. I'd have to run you in."

TROTTER WATCHED THE HORSES COME OFF THE FIRST turn and settle into the backstretch. Ground level is not the best place to watch this part of the race from. All you can see is a jumble of brown. Trotter squinted and looked for the baby-blue shirt worn by his jockey. He couldn't find it, and began flushing and chilling at the same time.

There's no need to panic, he thought. Maybe the jockey took his shirt off.

"What's going on back there?" Trotter asked Simpson.

Simpson usually charged two dollars to call the race from his lofty position, but he made an exception this time, since Trotter was an all right guy with his life on the line, and since Trotter didn't have two dollars.

"Your horse is on the outside, way outside," Simpson said.

"Stay on the track, please," Trotter said.

"He can't hear you," Looney said. "It's like sitting way up in the stands and yelling for a guy to score a touchdown. It's an exercise in futility."

"Shut up, damn it!" Reardon said to Looney.

When a horse goes outside, this means he has to cover more ground than a horse on the inside. When a horse is WAY outside, this can mean he's looking for a good spot to take a pee.

"There's two horses pulling away," Simpson said. "One of them's yours!"

The fine line that separates winning and losing was closing in around Trotter's neck. He was getting very warm. He yanked his colorful sport coat off and wadded it into a ball.

"They're gone," Simpson said.

The horses disappeared behind the tote board, together, like an airplane flying through the clouds. This breather enabled those at the rail a few moments of silent meditation. Those with elevated seats continued to talk to their horses and their jockeys, none of whom could hear. Few of the horses or jockeys understood English, anyway. As Marty had said, often, you bet an

American horse and a foreign jockey, there's going to be a communications gap. The last time Marty said that, a little jockey named Juarez offered to give Marty a toothless kind of communications gap.

The others along the rail were in varying states of disarray.

Evangeline, five bodies up the track, was cheering methodically for the four horse. She had plopped her two hundred on Star Gazer to show, and if it happened, she was looking at a profit of about a cool forty bucks. Sid Booten was slightly worried about the changes that would take place in the dear girl if she won. He silently wished the four horse would be struck by lightning. Here he *KNEW* what he was doing, what the numbers in the *Form* meant, what a big butt on a horse meant, and he had lost everything but his vocabulary. If Evangeline won her first time out, she would be hard to live with, if you can call kissing on the cheek after a date living. It was every man for himself out here. If God kept Evangeline's horse out of the money, Sid Booten swore to quit saving the centerfold from *Playboy.*

There is a simple reason the tracks around the country stagger their racing dates. It's kind of like a circus. The ticket sellers and cashiers rent apartments and follow the action. Jockeys make the circuit. There are few big-race conflicts among the major tracks. The reason for this is, God is only human. He can't be everywhere at once. He can only consider and process so many swears.

Vibes Eberhart was ALSO swearing to God as the horses went behind the tote board. He had bet on his most recent vibration, the same as Evangeline's, the four horse, and he had bet something grotesque, like a hundred dollars, to win, of course. Place and show betting are beneath contempt. If his horse won the feature, Vibes Eberhart swore to God never again to threaten his wife's life, beginning Monday.

Mickey Jax, who had tipped the four horse three times, was only swearing to God to give up drinking a particular brand of gin because, after all, he had tipped all the other horses and had insurance.

Jake the car park had become severely depressed at losing the Buick he thought was his, so he took the two-hundred-dollar pay-off from Trotter and bet it on the gray of this race, six. Jake swore to God that if this 6–1 shot came in, he would never again drive more than fifty miles per hour in the lot.

Solly Friedman was swearing to God to buy his wife a mink coat if that gray won. Then he took it back. It's hard following that act—picking two winners in a row. He'd get his wife a mink, anyway, the hell with the race.

Quinella Hogan was watching the race on the closed circuit TV set above her hamburger stand. She had bet the five dollars Trotter gave her on some dog that would enable her to make her cash register come out even. She swore to God never to short-change anybody she knew.

Even Lufkin swore to God. This place was making him nervous. He had only hung around in case Trotter won and wanted to shoot ten thousand or so on the night football game. Lufkin swore to God that if he could get out of this place with his four-hundred-dollar suit intact, he would seldom tell guys' wives how much their husbands were down.

About everybody at the rail around Trotter except those who hadn't bet—Looney, Miss Backstretch, Reardon, and Simpson—were more concerned with their own futures, so hardly anybody paid any attention when Trotter ripped a pocket off his new coat to use as a handkerchief.

It was definitely hard for Trotter to believe that a few hours ago he had been sitting on the concrete like a wino, awaiting the result of that first race. It felt like he had been here a week. Had he acted that way, had he just sat there in all that filth, like a bum? Impossible.

He also found it hard to believe, for a second, that he had bet a small but important fortune on this race. It was a good thing the horses ran from behind the tote board in the infield. When your horse is in the thick of it, there's no time to dwell upon life's little problems, like, "Am I insane?"

Simpson picked up his simple but accurate call of the feature.

"Where the hell's the rest of them?"

"Maybe they took a wrong turn," Looney said.

Two horses had pulled from the pack. The rest of them trailed behind like chaperones.

"They're pecker to pecker," Simpson said.

Trotter grabbed the rail, shook it, and asked, "Who?"

There are trees in the infield for some idiotic reason. As the leaders went into the final turn, it was like watching a race through a picket fence. Trotter had been there when one guy sitting in the infield tried to hang himself from one of these trees. Management thought that would be bad for business, so the lower limbs were cut off.

The official track announcer said over the loudspeaker, "Something, something, and a gap of ten lengths." It was hard to hear much.

Trotter looked at the tote board, which flashed the numbers of the leaders. No horse was listed for third place. The way it looked, *all* the horses were third.

"Ten lengths, hell," Simpson said. "It's about fourteen."

229

Two was listed as leading midway through the final turn, with number four in the box on the tote board reserved for second. Then the numbers were reversed: four, two. As Trotter watched the board, and the horses handled that last turn, the numbers of the leaders were switched twice more: two, four; four, two.

Two was Trotter's Hot to Trot.

Four was Star Gazer.

"There's nobody ahead," Simpson yelled. "Those two are dead-ass even!"

The track announcer put it more diplomatically.

Neck and neck, he said.

"Whoever has buckteeth wins," Simpson shouted, caught up in what would be reported in the major dailies as a "stirring stretch duel."

The writers, they bet, too, up there in the press box. They have a five-dollar window all their own. They get so excited that they hardly ever think of anything better than "stirring stretch duel."

"What a cruel joke it would be to lose so close a race after coming so far," Looney said.

Trotter didn't hear him. Nobody heard him.

Trotter and Pam had visited Niagara Falls once. The noise was like that now. The kids in the next motel room had screamed bloody murder all night. The water from the falls was fairly loud, too.

Reardon was standing to Trotter's left. He put his arm around Trotter's neck. Miss Backstretch was standing to Trotter's right. She put her arm around his waist. Trotter put his arms around both of their shoulders and yelled, so loud Looney jumped, "Oh, my God, *I'VE GOT IT!*"

Looney started to say it was still too early to tell, but, fearing for his life, he didn't. He *THOUGHT* it, though.

Simpson concluded his call of the race with, "Christ, they're glued together!"

Wouldn't it be just awful, Looney thought, to have a winner with so much riding on it disqualified for bumping or something?

Watching the last of it was like watching something familiar, Trotter thought, but what? It was like watching horses that galloped around an arena, stride for stride, with a beautiful woman standing with a foot on each horse's rump. *THAT* was what it was like, a trick.

You couldn't have shone a flashlight between the two leaders.

The rest of the horses were way up the track, giving their jockeys a Sunday ride a day early.

They ran that way, eyeball to eyeball, four and two, two and four, it was a matter of opinion. The track announcer tried hard to report the finish, but he, too, got lost in the excitement. He said, "At the wire, it's MY GOD!"

Trotter's heart missed a beat, or two, when the announcer said that. He thought a horse named My God had slipped in there somewhere. Trotter had watched the finish with the sleeve of his new coat clenched between his teeth.

He did not sit on the concrete this time. For one thing, Reardon and Miss Backstretch were holding him up.

Looney broke the silence and tension by hyperventilating. He began breathing in fast gulps and then he turned pale. Simpson picked a paper sack off the ground and had Looney breathe deeply, and although the sack smelled like Bourbon, Looney was his old self in a matter of seconds, and he said, "Thank God I am poor and don't have to worry about finishes like that."

Trotter had made two fists, and he hit them on the rail and said, "I knew it. I KNEW IT!"

He turned around and was smiling.

"Oh, honey," Miss Backstretch said.

Trotter reached out and squeezed her neck with his right arm.

"I told you, Reardon." Trotter put his left fist on Reardon's shoulder. "I DID know it."

How fickle, Looney thought. Furthermore, what the hell did he know?

Reardon opened his mouth to say something, but just couldn't, he was too exhausted. He bounced a fist off the rail. "We knew it," he said weakly.

The horses, four and two, two and four, managed to stop halfway into the first turn, they almost needed parachutes to slow them down, and they trotted back across the finish line to await the official decision. No protest had been flashed on the tote board.

"Just look at that," Simpson said. "Those two horses are walking, and they're still pecker to pecker."

The PHOTO light flashed on the tote board, and when it did, Trotter jumped in the air, right fist first, holding the receipt from his bet, and he let out a shout that scared the absolute hell out of the Dorns, who were standing five rows of bodies behind the strange goings on down there at the rail. They had been standing AT the rail, until some giant gave them thirty seconds to fall back.

This was Mrs. Dorn's first visit to the track.

Mrs. Dorn had had trouble understanding how much you won if you bet a horse to come in second and he came in first. It was the same amount you would win if you bet the horse to come in second and he came in second, but Mrs. Dorn was having trouble getting it straight.

When Mrs. Dorn had asked her husband just be-

232

fore the feature race why a horse paid less to show than it did to place, he had said in no uncertain terms that her incessant nagging was ruining his concentration. He had explained *EVERYTHING* a person needed to know on the way to the track. He had given her the right to ask one more question, before the feature, and, he said, it had better be a good one, or he would lose his wife in the crowd.

When the PHOTO light had gone on, when the guy swinging the weird jacket had jumped in the air and screamed with what was easily recognized as joy —even to the first-timer at the track—Mrs. Dorn tapped her husband on the shoulder.

"Okay, okay," her husband said. "What?"

"It's a photo finish, right?"

"Right," her husband said.

"The guy with the jacket had number two to win. I heard them talking. He bet a lot on number two."

"So?"

"In a photo finish, either horse can come in first, right?"

"Right. That's very good."

"So how does that guy down there *know* he won?"

"Beats me," Mr. Dorn said.

About the author . . .

Jay Cronley (1943-2017) was a humorist, novelist, third generation newspaper man, horse race correspondent, and for 46 years, a famed columnist in Tulsa, Oklahoma. During his decades at Tulsa World, he wrote more than 2,500 columns. His writing appeared in *Sports Illustrated, Playboy,* ESPN.com, and *Esquire.* Five movies were made from his books, including *Funny Farm* with Chevy Chase, *Quick Change* with Bill Murray, and *Let it Ride* with Richard Dreyfuss. He was a baseball star at the University of Oklahoma.

Another Jay Cronley book from Echo Point Books You May Enjoy

Funny Farm

The Farmers quit their jobs and move from New York City out to the country. But they have to share their rural paradise with wacky locals, marauding water snakes, and more hilarious gags and mishaps than they can shake a stick at...

"Uprorious . . . Uttlerly absurd . . . Wonderfully endearing."
—*The New York Times Book Review*

"Ridiculous, implausible, bonehead dumb, and laught-out-loud funny throughout"   —*Playboy*

PAPERBACK ISBN 978-1-63561-819-8

Our books may be ordered from any bookstore or online purveyor of books, or directly through our Web site, www.echopointbooks.com. Or visit our retail store, located in Brattleboro, Vermont.